The deepest feeling in me now is peace. I am quiet and still deep inside me, where there used to be a tremendous churning and shaking. So much lies ahead—not just my surgery, or my promised year with Simon, but something else even better; my future—a huge sweet thing, like the moon which is just coming up, silvery and shaped in the most excellent way. The brilliant globe rises straight over the waves, coming up with such certainty and power that we know that we can count on it for the rest of our lives.

Simon puts his forehead against mine, then presses his cheek against my cheek, then his nose against my nose, then his lips against my lips. I feel as if our faces fit into the face of the moon, perfectly.

We sit in the darkness and hold each other for a long time. We don't speak. We just *are*. After a while Simon rests his head against my shoulder and closes his eyes. With my finger I trace the shape of his eyebrows, feel the feathery curve of his eyelashes. I hear a song start in my heart: *You are the darling of my heart, stay till the moon goes down.*

Available from Crosswinds

Angel in the Snow
by Glen Ebisch

Lighten Up, Jennifer
by Kathlyn Lampi

Red Rover, Red Rover
by Joan Hess

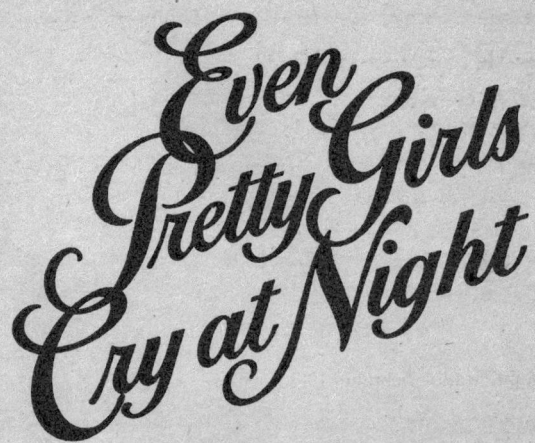

MERRILL JOAN GERBER

CROSSWINDS

New York • Toronto
Sydney • Auckland
Manila

First publication February 1988

ISBN 0-373-98017-5

Copyright © 1988 by Merrill Joan Gerber

All rights reserved. Australian copyright 1988. New Zealand copyright 1988. Philippine copyright 1988. Except for use in any review, the reproduction or utilization of this work in whole or in part in any form by any electronic, mechanical or other means, now known or hereafter invented, including xerography, photocopying and recording, or in any information storage or retrieval system, is forbidden without the permission of the publisher, Crosswinds, 300 East 42nd St., New York, N.Y. 10017

All the characters in this book are fictitious. Any resemblance to actual persons, living or dead, is purely coincidental.

Crosswinds is a registered trademark of the publisher.

Printed in the U.S.A.

RL 5.0, IL age 12 and up

MERRILL JOAN GERBER has published stories in *The New Yorker*, *The Atlantic*, *Mademoiselle*, *The Virginia Quarterly Review*, *The Sewanee Review* and elsewhere. Her story, "I Don't Believe This," first published in *The Atlantic*, was chosen for inclusion in *Prize O. Henry stories: O. Henry Awards 1986*. Besides numerous short stories, Ms. Gerber has published both adult and young adult novels. Among the latter are, *Please Don't Kiss Me Now* (Dial Press, NAL paperback), *Name a Star For Me* (Viking, NAL paperback), *I'm Kissing As Fast As I Can*, *The Summer of My Indian Prince*, and *Marry Me Tomorrow* (Fawcett). *Also Known As Sadzia! The Belly Dancer* is being published this April by Harper & Row.

Ms. Gerber holds an M.A. in English from Brandeis University. She has taught writing at universities, colleges and writers' conferences. She now lives in California and teaches at Pasedena City College.

Chapter One

"Crow" is the name they call me.

How the old people love to talk about me! "There goes the Crow," Yetta Korn whispered this afternoon to Bernie Kriegel as I passed by them, just as—when Marcia passed by—they whispered, "There goes the Beauty." *The Crow and the Beauty.*

Now it is night. I huddle on the very edge of the high diving board, staring down into the black, cold eye of the pool, waiting till it's safe for me to take flight. Crouched here on the quivering plank, I watch the lights in the windows of the cubicles click off, one by one, as the old people go to sleep. Of what do they dream? Do they dream of their past lives, when their husbands and wives were alive, still young and strong? Do they remember their children learning to walk and lifting up their little, dimpled hands? What is it like to be old and alone? Is it worse than being *young* and alone?

Sometimes I think Marcia and I are—to the old people—just a form of entertainment, like the checkers they play in the Game Room or the gin rummy cards they deal out in front of the cabanas. They have so little to do but watch us, wonder about us, whisper about us. Maybe they even envy us, the *"yingele"* (the Yiddish word they use for "young"). Marcia: the Olympic swimmer, the *"sheyn madele,"* the Beauty, and Faye: the unlucky bird, the *"umglicklich feygl,"* the Crow. Here, they observe us—right before their eyes each day, as constant as the sand and the ocean. Two young women, as different as day and night, living by some accident of fate among a hundred old souls in the Sea 'n' Surf Retirement Apartments.

Buzz, buzz, buzz, chatter, chatter, chatter. How they lean their heads together and talk about us as they sit in the plastic beach chairs around the pool and stare at us—me in my dark fluff of feathers slouching about, head down, gathering up wet towels and empty glasses, which is my job, and Marcia, dazzling as a hibiscus blossom on the high dive in her red Speedo swim suit.

Aah—at last, the light in Gertie Roth's room has gone out. She's always the last of the old people to give up the day. After her light goes out, only my father's light burns on, sending a small, bright rectangle onto the dark cement of the pool deck. I imagine Gertie wants to squeeze as many hours as she can get from each day. Secretly, I admire her. Of all the old people, she's the only one who tries to talk to me though I never answer her. "Hello, young lady," she always says, as I shuffle by in my hunch of feathers. "Such a hot day to wear that heavy jacket! What do you need it for, under this hot Miami sun? And how is your father?" she adds. "A pity about his leg." She never seems insulted when I don't reply. She always smiles at me, standing like a patient pigeon with her puffed out chest and her thin legs, waiting a few seconds before she walks along, on her way to the pool or the exercise room, as if one day I will actually answer her. But my policy is never to talk to the old folks here. If I talk to one, they'll all be giving me advice. So I keep my own counsel, as my father does his.

What a pair we are, my father and I—they call *him* the "Shadow," with his lame leg, his limp, his quiet ways; I watch them watching him as he shuffles about, fixing their sinks, their light switches, their leaking faucets. He paints their apartments (between tenants, often after someone has died), sees that their cabinets close, their doorbells buzz. What do they really think about him—that kind, handsome, soft-spoken, shy, lonely man? Well, I suppose we're quite a mystery to them. Father and daughter, Shadow and Crow. Hardly the all-American family. *How sad*, they must whisper to one another. *What a pity about his wife. What a pity about his leg. What a pity about his strange daughter.*

At last it is time. My father's light has not gone out, but it never does. He's certain to be asleep. I used to wonder if he slept with the light on because he was afraid—like me—of the dark. Now I know he is afraid. Often I hear him cry out in the night because he is having one of his nightmares. When I was eight or nine, I used to tiptoe into his room and lift his eyeglasses off his nose, take the book off his chest, shut off the lamp. But now I leave him alone, imagining the comforting glow of the light on his closed eyelids.

That is our unspoken pact—I leave him alone, he leaves me alone. Since I turned eleven, we have stayed separate in the ways that count, respecting each other's privacy. I never enter his bedroom, he never enters mine. What does he think about my dark feathery coat, the padded vault I wrap and hide myself in? He never asks, he never pries. He assumes correctly: if I do it, I must need to do it.

A few times I have almost told him—look, we are both crippled. We are soul twins. I have my own crippled life. Yours is from a land mine in Viet Nam, mine is from—God-knows-what. From my genes or maybe my evil thoughts; maybe it is a punishment, because once, when I was five, I screamed at my mother that I hated her.

Well, I am grateful he feels no need to question my habits. We get along, like two hermit crabs in a little tidepool. Life has offered my father a greater puzzle than this coat I wear. Why did my mother die so young? The greatest puzzle of all to him.

My time has come. The night is mine. The dark, private sky, the stars, the pool, the beach beyond—they are finally mine. Under my feet on the grainy board I can almost feel the shape of Marcia's delicate feet, her toes balancing just over the edge, getting ready for a perfect, exquisite dive. But this is her place only in the red glare of the sun, and it is mine in the dark of coming midnight.

Tall palms fan across the starry sky. The breeze rustles their fronds. I am invisible in the night—to be unseen is the gift the darkness gives to me. Finally I fling off my armor of feathers, letting my downy jacket fall to the cement below, and stand in my loose, black swimsuit. I stretch out my wings. I skitter my skinny bird feet to the edge of the board and take a strong perch from which to push off. My form is far from perfect. But I am used to myself—in the dark I can even love myself—and now I am about to set myself free. I count to three. I spread my wings and leap.

Chapter Two

In the early morning, I am drawn down the steps to the basement Game Room like a moth to a flame. It's dim and cool and smells strongly of cigar ash which, last night, the old men tapped off into the ashtrays on the card tables. I take pleasure in the acrid reek which stings my nostrils.

My body begins to burn (with envy or with the involuntary perspiration of a spy) the instant I see Marcia's graceful body. Her form is outlined by tiny, sun-filled air bubbles as she hurtles down through the gray-blue water of the pool, arcs upward and rises to the surface.

She is the fish, and I am looking into the fishbowl. The Sea 'n' Surf Retirement Apartments are famous for this one, amazing architectural miracle: its pool, carved out of the sandy loam of the beach, contains windows. Rather, they are like the portholes of an ocean liner, which look from the Game Room into the depths of the pool.

Yetta Korn, one of Gertie's friends whose airs suggest that she was at one time in her life a beauty queen, spends her time at the pool pretending she is Esther Williams, doing water ballet, wearing a bathing cap spiky with red rubber roses. She seems to hope that one of the old men playing pinochle in the Game Room will catch a glimpse of her through the portholes and take a passionate fancy to her. There are at least ten women to every man here; men just don't survive as long as women. Women, it seems, have to go on alone for a long, long time after their men die. It's a pity that's what women have to look forward to—except me, of course, or women like me—women who don't have to worry because they will always be alone.

Marcia cuts through the water to the surface. She is oblivious. Unless she comes right up to the portholes and peers through the double-thick glass, she cannot know she is being watched. Besides, Marcia has no reason to care who might be watching. Who would be watching who *counts*? The same people are always here—the old folks, or the Shadow, or the Crow. *No one* who counts. Marcia is unselfconscious; she swims in brightest daylight, training to become an Olympic star. She has only one thing on her mind when she swims, I am sure of it. To be better and better, until she is perfect.

But Marcia is already perfect. That's the irony of it. She has a flawless body, a beautiful face, a wedge of blond, gleaming hair. She has a spine as straight as an arrow, full breasts, powerful calves. She is *already* a star, a winner, a trophy-holder. She *can't* be luckier than she already is. Ask me. I know.

In the dimness of the Game Room, I lean my elbows on a card table as I read the headlines in yesterday's paper which someone left behind last night. Suddenly the overhead light ignites like a fire—a burst of fluorescent tubes flash across the ceiling, a line of tiny land mines.

"It's not good for your eyes, to be reading in the dark like this!"

Gertie Roth stands there smiling at me in the sun-bright glare. I shield my eyes, then wrap my jacket tighter about me. I am aware that in the fishbowl of the pool, the mermaid flutters her gorgeous tail.

"Your eyes are something you should take care of like precious jewels," Gertie says. "The young take it all for granted, that they can see, that they can walk."

I look down, at the broad, white ties of my tennis shoes. If Gertie is on her way somewhere, why doesn't she just keep going!

"Sometimes, darling," she says, "I worry that you'll get overheated in that jacket. It must be your favorite coat from when you lived in the snow. It's made of goosedown, isn't it? Did you use to live in the East? I'm from back East, maybe you can tell from the way I talk. Queens. My accent is Queens, not the Bronx. Not Brooklyn. There's a real difference, you know."

Go away, I think. *Go away now.*

"I got up early to do my exercises," Gertie says. "I want to get in shape for my seventeen-year-old grandson, Simon. He's coming next week to stay with me for the summer. How do you like that? My daughter sprang the whole thing on me like a jack-in-the-box! She calls up from Central Park West and says, 'Mama—how would you like company for the summer? Sam and I are going to visit Francie in Israel and get to know the new baby and we don't know where to park Simon. He doesn't want to go with us—you know how young people are about traveling with their parents. And alone here in New York he might get in trouble—so I thought, it's the perfect opportunity for him to get to know his grandmother better. And you could use company, couldn't you?'" Gertie taps me on the shoulder, and I jump away. "Does an old woman really know what to do with a teenage boy for two months? I'll go crazy! God forbid he should play rock and roll twenty-four hours a day. Maybe you can give me some ideas on what I can do with him."

I walk toward the shelves of games and begin straightening the boxes; Monopoly, Clue, Sorry, Trivial Pursuit. There are also twenty boxes of checkers and probably a hundred decks of cards. I keep my back to Gertie. I feel myself flushing inside my coat. I don't want her grandson here! She can't have him—he's not allowed. *Children are not allowed in this building.* Only I am allowed—I am the Shadow's daughter, after all; and Marcia is only allowed because her mother is the daughter of the Sea 'n' Surf's owner. But we don't need any teenage boys! That's absolutely certain!

"You'll meet him soon," Gertie says cheerfully. She fluffs her head of bouffant, blond curls. "You'll see—he's a nice boy, he has a sweet personality. His looks I can't vouch for these days—I haven't seen him in five years—but I can tell you one thing. When he was a baby, he had the most adorable dimples in his tush."

I am thinking I must have my father talk to Gertie and set her straight. No children, no teenagers, are allowed in this retirement condominium, least of all noisy young men! My father has to see that the rules are obeyed, he's the manager, after all, the custodian, the carpenter, the sergeant at arms. We will get this straightened out once and for all.

"You like my hairdo, darling?" Gertie asks me.

She's trying to trick me into talking. I never waver in my resolve. I *never* talk to the old people.

"You *should* like it, it cost a fortune." She pulls off her hair in one motion as if it is a wad of yellow cotton. "Surprise!" Underneath is a flat cap of her own thin, white hair. Her pink scalp shows through. I realize she is very old, much older than I thought. The skin over her temples is nearly transparent, veined with blue, pulsing with the thump of her heart.

"Did I shock you? It's just a wig, sweetheart! Why should I fuss with hair dye which can give you cancer and hot curlers which can burn your hair right off when all I need to do to look gorgeous is to plop on a wig?"

She waits for me to laugh, at least to respond. I bow my head and shuffle away. Gertie is never daunted. She calls after me, "Have a nice day, darling. One of these days, whenever you feel like it, we'll have a little chat. But remember, always make sure you read by a good light. Your eyesight is precious. Your whole body is precious. Whatever we get in life, that's what we get, so we have to take care of it."

Chapter Three

I know one thing. Gertie's accent isn't "Queens." It's something strange and foreign, despite her jaunty tone. There's a low, guttural sound to some of the words she speaks as if they're not really the words she's saying, but instead have some secret, dark meaning. I'm good at knowing about secrets; my whole life is a secret. Sometimes I'm amazed at girls who seem as if they never have secrets, never have anything private or shameful or strange to hide. Girls like Marcia seem that way; everything about them is out in the open—their bodies, their voices, their desires. I can't even begin to imagine a life that's all out in the open, all surface!

Yetta Korn is right in the middle of the pool, exactly in Marcia's way. Today Yetta is wearing a bathing cap with plastic cherries on it. They sound like the rattle of a rattlesnake as she tosses her head this way and that, doing her crazy water ballet.

"Hey Yetta," Marcia calls from her position on the high dive. She is standing right in the center of the sun; she is blinding, dazzling. She shimmers in my vision. Yetta flails around like a cow who accidentally slipped into the water.

"What sweetheart? What can I do for you? You want me to teach you this step?"

"Could you move out of my way?" Marcia's voice is strong; she is clearly annoyed but resigned for the moment. She knows she can't have the pool to herself at midday. It's just one of those things she has to put up with till she can get what she wants. I have a feeling that one day Marcia will be mistress of her own mansion, her own pool—like the pools in those houses on Seashore Drive, houses with iron gates and guard dogs and Cadillacs in the driveway. Marcia is the kind of girl who knows exactly what she wants and how to get it. Where does that kind of assurance come from?

Yetta moves out of the way, her cherries clacking. Marcia does a perfect dive. She comes up and shakes her short, blond hair like a dog, spraying water in every direction. She breast-strokes toward the shallow end and comes up the steps. Whenever Marcia comes out of the pool, the water just rolls off her as if she's made of plastic. A plastic woman. Nothing seems to get to her, to get *into* her. Maybe that's what they mean by the saying "Like water off a duck's back." Nothing penetrates, nothing pierces, nothing *hurts*!

Now Gertie Roth appears, coming up the stairs from the Game Room. She's wearing her purple bathing suit with a rainbow stripe. She waves to Yetta Korn. Yetta Korn is trying to get the attention of Bernie Kriegel; she's doing back flips and pointing her toes skyward under his nose. But Bernie's nose is buried in the *Wall Street Journal*, and he only sits near the pool so he can flick bits of cigar ash into it. Plastic people—Yetta and Bernie.

I don't know about Gertie Roth—anyone as cheerful as she is is probably a plastic person, too.

"Yoo-hoo," Gertie calls to Yetta. "You ready for canasta, Yetta? I got Wheat Thins and mozzarella and green olives for a little snack."

"Give me two minutes," Yetta calls back, clacking her cherries. "I have four more cartwheels in my routine."

"Don't drown yourself," Gertie says. "No lifeguard on duty here."

"Bernie can always save me," Yetta says pointedly, batting her eyelashes in Bernie's direction. Bernie rattles his newspaper. All I can see of him from the row of cabanas where I'm working is the top of his bald head, the newspaper and his veiny, sinewy legs.

I go about my business, changing the towels in the cabanas, emptying ashtrays, sweeping up sand from the shower stalls. I feel like Cinderella—doing the dirty work while Marcia stands outlined against the sun, every drop of water on her body sparkling like a diamond.

She doesn't *need* to have a job, her grandfather owns the Sea 'n' Surf Retirement Apartments. Her mother's divorced and spends her time on the beach, improving her tan. When they go out shopping on Lincoln Road, two blond, tanned, beautiful women, they always come back with bags and boxes from the best shops.

I can imagine my father and me shopping together on Lincoln Road. The Shadow and the Crow—just the pair to be into high fashion. We'd probably peer through the windows until some security guard asked us to leave.

My father still has his Viet Nam boots in which he marched through rice fields—thick black leather boots that go up over his ankles. Sometimes he polishes them—he never wears them, but leaves them standing on a little table in the hall, in the same place other people would have a pretty lamp or a vase with flowers. If he needs to leave me a note, he leaves it for me in one of the boots.

He's no crazier than anyone else. I love my father. He's the saddest man in the world. He's sweet and he has nightmares at night, and I know he misses my mother more than even I do. But we just don't talk. We get along, but that's about all. That's fine with me. What could we talk about? My school work? Why I don't have friends? Why I wear my down jacket all the time?

It's fine this way. I help him around the Sea 'n' Surf, and I work at the front desk sometimes, distributing mail into the boxes, handling cabana rentals, keeping an eye on things. The Sea 'n' Surf used to be a fancy hotel long ago, which is why it has cabanas all around the pool. People who don't have pools of their own, mostly middle-aged women, rent the cabanas—which gives them pool privileges and a place to shower and change.

I like to work in the cabanas. They have cool cement floors which are sandy and sometimes damp. The cabanas smell slightly of salt air. All I have to do each morning is fill pitchers with ice water, set out plastic cups, put clean towels on the racks. There are days that even the rented cabanas are empty, that no one comes to swim, and on those days I often take one for my own use, close the door, and sit on a lounge chair in the dimness, writing poems. If I leave the door open a crack, I can see a line of brilliant sunlight, see through the crack to the outside world, see Marcia doing her dives, see Gertie eating her Wheat Thins, see Bernie reading the stock market reports, see Yetta's red cherries.

This is the poem I wrote today:

There are no pictures of my mother holding me;
In the leather picture album, my father holds me everywhere; at fireworks, on ponies, deep in snowdrifts,
on a carousel with caramel apples on our double lap as we ride on,
the shadow of his pipe our hot connection.
But where are my mother's arms around me?
Nowhere, nowhere.
Her lesson is as clear to me as the empty sky:
We live and die alone.

Chapter Four

He's here! This is unbelievable! Gertie's grandson is here, right under my nose! I can see him this very minute from my bedroom window. He's standing at the fence at the end of the pool near the ocean, leaning forward, his arms on the wooden top rail. He's staring at the ocean as if he owns it—*my* ocean. I can't see his face, but he's got light, curly hair, a tall, thin body. Something about the way he stands almost makes my heart stop. I don't want to have to deal with this! My life is already hard enough. This is intolerable.

How dare she! The nerve! How could Gertie have let him come, especially after I went up to her apartment last week and slid under her door a copy of the *Agreement Between Tenants and the Sea 'n' Surf Re-*

tirement Apartments. How could she dare to go against the rules!

I especially circled clause Four of the contract which is as clear as crystal: *Tenants agree that no minors will reside in the apartment complex. (Exclusions to the rule apply only to Henry Marcus, Manager, and his daughter, Faye, and to Florence King and her daughter, Marcia.)* Gertie *couldn't* have missed that clause because I put a big, red star in the margin, circled the whole thing in red and wrote a warning note to her, forging my father's name. The note was a little masterpiece, I thought:

Dear Mrs. Roth:
My daughter, Faye, tells me that you have been considering having as a guest for the summer your teenage grandson. Let me remind you that it is the policy of the Sea 'n' Surf to have no children residing on the premises for any reason, an agreement you signed when you signed your original lease. For your comfort as well as that of the other guests who crave a peaceful and restful environment, you can, I am sure, appreciate the good sense of this policy. You have been an excellent tenant, and I trust you will continue to be one by abiding by the rules of the management.

Henry Marcus,
Manager

Forging—just a little talent I picked up for survival when I found out I had to take phys ed in ninth grade. Nothing in the *world* was going to get me into those showers with twenty other girls. They weren't going to force me into those little gym suits—short white shorts and a tank top with Flamingo High School stamped on it in big, green letters. Then my back would have been right out in the open for everyone to gaggle at. And I certainly wasn't going to appeal to my father to get me out of phys ed. How could he, anyway? He didn't even *know* his daughter was shaped like a corkscrew—he doesn't know to this day.

And it was so easy to forge the letter. I can see how easy it would be to become a criminal. A little forging. A little stealing. In my position—since the master key to every apartment in the building hangs right on a nail in our kitchen cabinet—it would be quite simple.

But all I ever stole in my entire life was one piece of stationery from the desk of eighty-six-year-old Herman Brugman, retired M.D., who used to live on the fourth floor. He used to keep a pile of his old stationery as scratch paper beside his telephone.

"To Whom It May Concern..." I wrote under the letterhead which read:

DR. HERMAN BRUGMAN
SPECIALIST IN
PULMONARY MEDICINE

My patient, Faye Marcus, has a chronic and serious asthma condition. Participating in sports may serve to bring on a life-threatening attack. Therefore, I require that she be excused from physical education classes for the remainder of her years in high school. Thank you.

                        Dr. Herman Brugman

For a while I was afraid the school nurse would call Dr. Brugman's old office phone number to double-check, but no one ever inquired into his diagnosis, and he died of a coronary when I was a junior last year.

Asthma. I wish I had something that simple. A girl in my math class has it and she brings an atomizer with her in her purse and now and then she inhales some medicine from it. In two seconds she feels fine. Why can't I take one deep breath of some magic spray and in two seconds be free of my agony?

God, there's something so beautiful about him, Gertie's grandson. Just by his stance I can tell he loves it here—the way he puts his foot on the lower railing and leans his forearms on the upper one. It's the way a guy might put his foot up into his girlfriend's car if he were leaning on her car door talking to her while she sat inside.

He's going to make this place his own. I can tell. He'll probably start swimming at night, which is my time. He might start talking to the old folks and find out things he'd be better off not knowing. He might...God, I know he will...fall in love with Marcia.

No! He can't stay here! He can't! I won't allow it! Rules are rules. We all have to live by rules. The world runs by rules, traffic rules, going to school rules, taking phys ed rules. Who are Gertie and her grandson that they think they can break the rules of this place without consequences? He's so handsome, standing out there with the wind billowing his shirt. I can't bear to think of a summer of looking at him, with his light hair curling into the sun, and his strong legs walking on the sand... walking next to Marcia. *For what on earth else could possibly happen?*

So I'm crying now. So what? I'm entitled to cry, I don't do it very often, and it's perfectly safe and private here, with Daddy out somewhere in the bowels of the building with his toolbox.

Do I have a right to cry? Let's be sure. Let me cry at least for the right reasons—let me be honest. Let me not cry because Gertie's grandson is handsome or because he's so sweet and decent looking; let me not cry because Marcia has everything in the world a girl could want—a mother, for one thing. Beauty, health and money for the others. And soon she'll have this wonderful grandson of Gertie's, too. Forget all that and let me cry for the real reason.

I unbutton my blouse and throw it on the bed. Then I take the hand mirror and turn my back to my long dresser mirror. I hold the mirror up and there I am. *That's* what I'm entitled to cry about.

My back is completely off kilter, out of synch, totally screwed up. My left shoulder is two inches lower than my right shoulder. My left hip sticks way out, sharp as an elbow, and my right hip is skewed inward. On the right side of my back beside my twisted spine is a great ugly rib hump. The hunchback of Notre Dame has nothing on me. I'm a freak. I belong in the side show of some circus. I grew crooked, like a sunflower that had to bend around a hard, misplaced rock. But the rock is inside me. The rock *is* me. So I think I'm entitled to cry.

But now I can't. Grief is stuck inside me like a thorn. The pain won't move up or down; it tries to pierce my heart. But a rock doesn't give up tears or blood. It sits, stony and dead, for all eternity.

I get impatient with myself. Now that I can't cry after all that, I feel bored with my misery. I toss down the mirror, throw on my blouse, take a drink of grapefruit juice in the kitchen, comb my wavy brown hair in the bathroom.

On a sudden impulse, I pick up a pair of scissors from a shelf in the medicine cabinet and begin to hack off my hair. I'm not crazy; I really don't feel crazy. Yet this seems to be a crazy thing to do. I no longer want my ordinary, brown, wavy, shoulder-length hair. I no longer want this plastic barrette pulling it back from my face. I want to make a drastic change. *I have to!* If I can't make it in my life, in my body, in my hopes—I can at least make it in my hairstyle.

So wham—I'm just whacking it right off. Even as the long strands fall into the sink, the crown of hair on my head puffs out, fluffs out, lighter than it was before. I stick my head under the faucet and let a flood of water soak through to my scalp. Though my hair was jagged looking dry, it's like magic when I wet it, it begins to curl up all around my head. Not so bad. I adjust it here and there, snipping and clipping away. I get it pretty even all around. Well, what a change. I don't look like the same person. It's a start. But of what? What am I doing to myself? The Crow, the *umglicklich feygl*, the unlucky bird, is getting a new look. My heart skips a beat. What if this is a terrible mistake, what if I'm sorry I ever did it?

Chapter Five

"Look at the glamour girl!" Yetta Korn shouts from the center of the pool where she's kicking like a maniac, creating a frothy whirlpool. "Darling, I love your new hairdo—you look like Barbra Streisand."

Ignore her.

I keep my head down, check to see that the zipper of my jacket is zipped to the top. I go from table to table, a raggedy towel in my hand, a trash bag looped over my arm to catch the cracker crumbs, the cigar stubs, the crumpled tissues. I don't get paid for this job; it's just my job. If I didn't do it my father would have to do it; but he does everything else. It's only fair that I help him, though he doesn't require me to. He doesn't require anything of me. Sometimes he looks at me as if he's baffled about how I got there, into his house, into his life. He sometimes looks at me with the saddest look, as if he has no idea what to do with me. Not that he doesn't love me—I think he does, very much, but he doesn't know what to do with love anymore. The first time, he gave everything to my mother and he was betrayed. I sometimes think of all those months he was in Viet Nam, dreaming of coming home to my mother, having that as the vision that kept him going through the jungles, through the rice fields—and then, she slipped away from him, she died, just like his friend Jim Ransome, the medic, who slipped out the door of the medevac helicopter as it was evacuating wounded, and died of a broken neck.

Somehow my father just manages, like the rest of us, to go on. He gets up at dawn and tests the pool with his little kit of chemicals. In the Pool House, a little tin storage building with a locking door situated at the side of the pool, he keeps his equipment: the skimmer, the pool vacuum, the plastic bottles of chlorine, the powdered acid, the diatomaceous earth for the filter. All day and night the motor hums, keeping the pool water shimmery clean and blue, filtering out petals from Yetta Korn's rubber roses, straining out leaves, sand, hair, algae. The pool heater thumps and hums to keep the pool temperature an even eighty-two degrees.

Diatomaceous earth, the stuff that clings to the filter and acts as a superfine strainer, fascinates me. In the big metal tub my father keeps it in, it looks like white sand, but it's really the bodies of little calcified sea creatures, ground to a fine powder.

Diatoms. Creatures which live in the depths of the salty, green sea while whales pass overhead blocking out the sun, and octopi shoot past. To come to this: to be destined, as pulverized grains, to strain out Yetta's fake flower petals!

"Listen, don't listen to what Yetta says, Sweetiepie," Bernie Kriegel calls over his newspaper. "You don't look like Streisand; she's never done anything for me. You look like one of those gorgeous poodles...."

"That comparison she won't like," Yetta warns him.

"I'm only kidding around," Bernie says. "You look plain gorgeous, forget the poodles."

I just keep wiping the tables. Ignoring them.

I hear them whispering. Yetta had flapped and flopped her way to the edge of the pool, just under his skinny shins. They whisper—but they're loud. "The Crow," I hear Yetta say. "She's a troubled girl. Maybe you shouldn't try to kid around with her."

"A good laugh would loosen her up," Bernie says. Then they start to talk in Yiddish. I don't care if they talk in Chinese. Do they think I care what they say about me?

I catch a glimpse of myself in the silver side of the water fountain. Distorted by the bent metal. But then, I always look distorted. My hair was much better long. Then it could hang over my face and hide my eyes. Why hadn't I left it alone?

My face isn't so bad, actually. Maybe I wanted it to show. Maybe I wanted Gertie's grandson to see it. I have a nice face; on someone else it might even be called a pretty face. On Marcia, it would even be called a lovely face. But then on Marcia, anything would be lovely. A witch's mask would be lovely. A cobra's head would be magnificent.

When I pass the water fountain, I bend down pretending to wipe the sides and glance at my reflection. My blue eyes have no hint of hunchback; my nose is nicely shaped and perfectly regular; my lips are full and smooth. My smile—well, who knows? Maybe I have a curvature of the smile. Why find out? I never smile, and I'm not going to smile here, in public, where someone could see me.

"Excuse me," says a voice. It's not the voice of Bernie or Yetta. It's none of the old folks. It's a voice I never heard. My heart turns over.

I keep wiping the silver case of the water fountain with my towel till it glows.

"Excuse me," the voice says again. I know by the goose bumps on my back who it is. I don't stop wiping, I don't turn my head.

He has the nerve to tap me on the shoulder. I jump up as if he tried to electrocute me.

"Oh! I'm sorry," he says. "I didn't mean to startle you."

I stand up and face him. I mean to scowl, to narrow my eyes, to fix him with my beady little crow eyes. But instead—astonishingly—I smile. My fists are clenched, but I smile into the eyes of Gertie's grandson.

"I'm Simon," he says genially, holding out his hand. "It's a real relief to see someone here my own age."

I twist the towel in both my hands, not daring to shake his.

"Can't you see I'm busy?" I say. "I have work to do here."

He looks surprised at my curt tone after that smile, which he can't know was totally involuntary.

"Well, actually I'm looking for the manager. I'd like to talk to him, and Gertie Roth—she's my grandmother, you know—she said you might know where I could find him. She said he's your father."

"He's busy, too."

Simon shrugs. "I didn't mean I have to see him right now. Maybe later when it's convenient, I'd like to ask him a question...a favor, really."

"What kind of favor?"

"Well, Gertie says there's a storeroom in the basement and she thought maybe I could use it. I'm thinking of building—well, I want to build a dulcimer, it's a kind of musical instrument, you know. And Gertie doesn't want me getting sawdust all over her apartment."

"The Storeroom is for storage," I say curtly.

Simon blinks his eyes (the same color blue as mine), and I see he is beginning to get the message. He looks as if I've slapped him. I feel a weird, sad twinge somewhere in my stomach. After all, he hasn't turned the knife in me... he hasn't done a thing to me. What have I got against him? Well, he hasn't turned it *yet*. Give him time.

As if fate has read my mind, I hear Yetta call out in her fake stage whisper to alert Bernie. "A little soap opera, Bernie, could be starting here. There comes the *sheyn madele*!"

The Beauty.

Well, it was only a matter of time. The sooner we get this over with, the better.

Marcia comes parading down the pool deck wearing her red Speedo swim suit. A yellow towel is slung over her shoulder. Her round breasts are beautiful, shimmering as she walks, and the outline of her nipples are perfectly visible. She walks like a princess, as if she owns the earth. It's clear she owns the sun, too, the way it shines so lovingly on her golden hair, the way it illuminates the fine down on her upper thighs.

Simon is dumbstruck. Who wouldn't be? His mouth hangs open as she promenades toward the high dive, tosses her towel over a lounge chair. She absently rubs a place on her ankle and then starts her easy rapid climb up the metal ladder, sliding her hands in smooth lines along the railing. She walks out on the diving board with perfect balance, wiggles her toes into place at the edge, swings her arms back and executes a perfect, arrowlike dive, deep into the clean, shimmery water of the pool.

Simon lets out his breath.

"Wow," he says. "She's really something, isn't she?"

I'm thinking of something cutting and nasty to say, like "She does it every day, it's nothing to her." But it doesn't half express what I'm feeling. I get my mouth ready, trying to summon the appropriate thought, the appropriate, indifferent, nasty remark—and suddenly I feel a hot wave rise up from my shoulders, flow through my neck, creep over my face and spill out into my eyes. Tears! I don't believe this! I'm crying. Because of some stupid girl doing some stupid, mindless dive.

I turn away from Simon and rush down the steps into the Game Room. Crying! In public! Worse even than smiling in public. Something is getting to me, breaking down my defenses. I rush past a group of four ladies setting up their canasta game. I know every one of them, their names, what they wear, their diets, their illnesses. They know nothing about me. They don't even look at me.

I think they're lucky to be so old. I wish I were old. I wish I were ancient and shriveled and deaf and blind. No—even that won't do. What I really wish is that I were dead!

Chapter Six

At dinner my father and I both read issues of *National Geographic*. I read an article about the Chinese expedition to Mount Everest, during which the only woman ever to attempt to climb the mountain stepped backward to let her partner go by and fell to her death. I wonder why she was so polite. Maybe women should be less polite and not worry about giving other people room. Her name was Marti; half a man's name. If someone had to fall, why was it the only woman on the expedition? It makes you wonder. Women are always so aware of what other people need, always trying to arrange that everyone gets what he wants. Which is exactly why I *don't* want Simon to get to use the Storeroom. Why should I arrange for it just because it's what he would like? Do I get what I want just because I would "like" it? He's already broken the rules by moving in here. It seems quite apparent no one is going to do anything about it.

I mentioned this to my father, and all he did was raise his puzzled blue eyes to me and shrug. "Why make trouble? Gertie is a nice woman," he said. "The boy seems nice. It's only for the summer. And who knows—maybe it will be nice for you to have someone young around."

That's what my father said; that's how out of it he is. "Maybe it will be nice for you!" If my mother were alive she'd have understood at once; someone young and handsome would *not* be nice for me to have around! Not when Marcia is also around! A woman would have understood at once.

In some ways, my father has no sense. He's not sensitive to what other people are feeling. Sometimes I think my father is like a poor, soundless farm animal, without the gift of thought or speech, grazing, never looking forward, hardly feeling anything inside his thick hide.

See how he eats what I cook and never even tastes it? Spaghetti tonight, and garlic bread. With real grated Parmesan cheese. I could serve TV dinners every night, and he'd never notice. It just worked out this way—I'm the female in the household, so I cook. I don't really mind cooking that much, it gives me something to do when we're both in the apartment together. I'd rather cook than watch television with my father—he watches whatever is on. He hardly seems to see the screen. What a strange household this is, what a sad stew we eat here every night.

* * *

"Want to see where I'd like to live?" my father asks. I look up at once because he rarely talks to me. He pushes the magazine toward me across the table, spinning it around so it will be right side up to my sight. I am really astonished—he so rarely initiates any discussion. On the page is a little stone cottage on a green field in Ireland. Great lowering gray clouds fill the sky, a few cows graze in the distance.

There! I knew it. My father wants to live like a cow, peacefully existing, never exerting himself, never concerning himself with the future, the past, consequences.

"Would you like to live there?" he asks.

"With you?"

"No, I don't mean that. Just live there."

"Alone? By myself?"

"Or with someone. Whatever you want."

I have a sudden vision of myself in the doorway of that stone cottage, and I see, coming toward me along a path in the field...walking over the lush green grass...the figure of...Simon! Of all people! Simon, with his thin body bent into the wind, his light hair blowing, the planes of his cheeks catching the light.

"I don't know," I say, feeling alarmed. "No. Not especially. Why would I want to live in the middle of nowhere? I'm perfectly happy here."

"I just thought this kind of place would please you," my father says. "I thought you like privacy. It seems as if it would suit you."

* * *

In bed at night I think of what would happen to me if my father and I moved to Ireland. Maybe I would become a Catholic and join a convent. I would join an order that still used heavy wool habits, not one of the modern ones whose members now dress in street clothes. No one would question my heavy layers of clothing then, no one would dare to. And the question of men would be resolved, too. I would never have to think about being in love, never think about marrying. Clothing and men, my two great problems, out of the picture.

But I'm not religious. And I couldn't take sacred vows simply because of men and clothing. I have to think of other alternatives: joining a cult, joining the U.S. Navy, joining the Peace Corps. No matter what I joined, I'd still have to be there, in my body, in my mind. I am stuck with myself. Though I have always known this, putting it into words depresses me.

I turn on the clock radio beside my bed and listen to the sad songs of Schubert on the classical music station. I don't know a word of German, but the songs are so sad, I feel I've written them myself. They're about terrible pain and suffering. Love and loss. Maybe people used to suffer *then*, in Schubert's day. I don't know one person in my real life who suffers. My father doesn't suffer—he's hardly conscious. Gertie Roth doesn't suffer—all she thinks about is her wig, her exercises, her card games. Bernie Kriegel doesn't suffer—all he does is worry about how the stock market is doing. Yetta Korn is a joke. How can a rubber flower suffer? And of course there's Marcia. Marcia, the Beauty. The idea of Marcia and suffering in the same thought is laughable. She's the eternal "what—me worry?" girl. Her biggest problem in life has probably been a broken fingernail. Her mother, Florence King, sometimes looks a little sour when she goes out to the beach every morning, but whatever is annoying her isn't in a category with real suffering. She charges out into the sunshine every morning with her big purple towel, her paperback book, her manicure tools, her case of nail-polish bottles. Her main interest in life seems to be her suntan. She oils her body and turns back and forth on the towel as if she's cooking herself through and through.

Well, let's try Simon, put him to the test. What could he know of suffering? A young, good-looking boy without a care in the world! Can he possibly know how much more his presence here is increasing *my* suffering?

My anger flares again. He has no right here! Rules are rules. Simon and his grandmother shouldn't be permitted to get away with this! Gertie, especially. What gives her the right to think she can blithely go through life, ignoring the rules of the house?

Well, I'm not going to let her get away with it! Since my father won't do anything about it, I will! Someone has to tell off people who take advantage. I will take action! Comforted by the thought, I turn off the radio, turn off the light and go to sleep.

"Who is it?" Gertie's voice sings out. "If it's not a mugger, just a second, I'll be right there."

She opens the door with a flourish. I don't have to worry about Simon's being in the apartment; I was careful to be certain he was out walking on the beach before I came up here.

"What a surprise!" Gertie cries when she sees me. She's wearing a little white terry-cloth jumpsuit and she's breathing hard. Beads of perspiration are on her wrinkled forehead. "What a pleasure! I'm always so happy to see a little bird at my door. Come in, darling. I was just riding my Exercycle, so excuse how I'm out of breath. My doctor says it's good for my cardiovascular, so I'm doing it. I'd rather be dancing, but since I have no partner to dance with, I'm pedaling. You do what you can in this world."

I hold out another copy of the *Agreement Between Tenants and the Sea 'n' Surf Retirement Apartments.*

"Let me get my glasses," Gertie says. But then she says, waving her hand at the paper, "Never mind—I know what you're giving me. Who needs so many legal forms, *Feygele*? Now I have three! What are you planning to be, a lawyer? All the small print gives me a headache."

She takes the contract from my hand and puts it down on an embroidered tablecloth covering her little kitchenette table. "Rules, rules, rules," she says. "Sometimes, to survive, you ignore the rules. You have to."

I turn to go. I'm not going to talk to her, I don't talk to the old folks and I'm not going to start now. She knows what I'm here for. That's what's important.

"Don't run away so fast. I was just going to have a nice cup of tea and some *mandelbrot*. Sit, it couldn't hurt you to have a delicious snack. You could gain a little weight, a little meat on those bones wouldn't hurt you."

Before I can move, she pulls out a chair, sits me down. She wears gold bracelets on both arms, and they ring and clatter upon one another as she sets out pretty teacups, saucers, a little dish of sugar cubes. How vain, I think, for someone to be covered with gold jewelry in their own house, early in the morning.

"Give me one second, and the teapot will be whistling." She rushes off into the kitchen and leaves me there, looking into a delicate china cup which has a single pink rose painted on the bottom.

I look around the room. I see a duffle bag beside the fold-out couch—it must be Simon's. I see a photograph in an ornate brass frame on the windowsill of the window which looks out onto the pool. I get up and go to look at it.

It's a very old picture, all sepia tones and ragged edges, but the frame is elegant. It looks as if it were just polished this morning. In the picture is a beautiful young woman, standing, holding an infant—a baby girl. The child is in a long, white dress with a high lace neck. Beside the woman, sitting in a chair, is a handsome, smiling young man. If I talked to the old folks, I'd ask Gertie whose family that was. The young woman looks almost like a younger, thinner, more peaceful Gertie—there's something about the eyes, the mouth. I glance at Gertie. But the young woman has a great dark mass of hair wrapped gracefully into a bun, and when I look at Gertie all I can see is her wig of blond glittery curls.

She has come out of the kitchen carrying a shining teapot. A little trail of steam is wafting out of the hole in the lid, giving off a weak little whistling sound. When she sees me standing before the picture, she starts to talk even faster than usual.

"Come, sit over here, quick, while the tea is hot. You know the saying, don't you? 'Hot tea will cure whatever ails you.' Why they invented iced tea is beyond me. It's like eating cold stuffed cabbage. It's pointless. All the beauty is lost."

I don't come to the table. I don't want her hot tea. Tea can't fix what ails me. I stand looking at the photo of the woman, the man and the baby till Gertie rushes over to me and suddenly turns the picture facedown.

"Full of dust," she says, her voice sounding funny. "This I will dust the first chance. When company is here, I shouldn't have dusty pictures all over my house." She points out the window. "Well, look at that. The Beauty is wearing a new bathing suit today." Clearly she is trying to distract me. She seems worried that I'll ask her about who's in the picture. But she doesn't have to worry. I don't intend to say a word.

The Beauty is wearing some pearly-white little thing today, no more red Speedo swimsuit, but a tiny bikini. Is this in Simon's honor? I'm sure it is. There she goes, hippety-hop, up the steps of the high dive.

And lo and behold, there's Simon, the young man my father thinks will give me so much pleasure by his presence. He's right there, at the foot of the ladder, looking up at her. She pauses at the top, leans her head down so that the sun sparkles off her crown and addresses a few words to him. So he and Marcia have met. What did I expect? That they never would? Idiot that I am, I prayed they would never meet. Or that I would meet him first. That he and I would...

Gertie, standing beside me (she's really much shorter than I am, no more than five feet tall), suddenly puts her arm around my waist—or wherever my waist would be if I weren't wearing my down jacket.

"Darling," she says. "Maybe I know what you're thinking. Maybe I know you think that girl out there has nothing in the world to worry about. But let me tell you something. You can believe me or not, whatever you want. But it's true what I'm going to tell you. You may not believe it now, but one day you'll know I'm telling you the truth. Even pretty girls cry at night. Even the Beauty. Life is no picnic for anyone."

Chapter Seven

Clearly, Bernie Kriegel is courting Yetta Korn. He's been giving her all his empty brown plastic cigar holders, and she's strung them on a black velvet ribbon and is wearing them around her neck. She looks like some kind of weird native, wearing the teats of a cow or the teeth of some extinct animal. She and Bernie carry on at the pool like newlyweds—she does her ballet like a hippopotamus in the water, blowing him kisses, and he takes a new cigar out of its holder, smells it and waves the case as an offering to Yetta.

"Come and get it, Sweet Lips!"

She breast-strokes to the side of the pool, and he hands her the tube; she rinses it in the pool, and a few tiny flecks of tobacco dust the surface of the water.

They will have to be strained out by the diatoms. I decide that in college I may study to be an anthropologist. My field of study will be Miami Beach. Since I'm not going to be a nun, I might as well choose something interesting to do. Some anthropologists go to study the culture of Java or Bali or the jungles of Africa or Australia, but I have all I need right here at the Sea 'n' Surf. The old folks here constitute a separate and unique culture.

Gertie is all dolled up in her wig and some fancy Lucite shoes that have little flecks of gold embedded in them. She's setting up for a game of canasta with some of her lady friends. I see she's watching out of the corner of her eye the carryings-on of Bernie and Yetta. Maybe she's jealous. Maybe in her heart she would love to have Bernie for a dancing partner. Maybe Yetta is to Gertie as Marcia is to me—the Beauty who gets the handsome prince. It's like what we learned in algebra: X is to Y as A is to B. Funny how you can apply these ideas to what's going on at the pool at the Sea 'n' Surf!

There are so few eligible men around here for the women. There are so few men who can even *walk*! There's old Mr. Bernstein, who leans on his cane and walks one step every five minutes; there's Henry Rubin who is tall and thin and completely bald. He's always chewing mints. Bernie, even with his sinewy, veiny legs, seems the most virile and energetic. He seems to have a real interest in life—or at least in two things in life: the stock market and Yetta Korn.

I go about my duties at the pool. When I get to the canasta table, there's already a full ashtray, filled by Sadie Gorman, a tall woman who always wears accordion-pleated dresses with palm trees on them. She has emphysema and knows she shouldn't smoke. I guess it's more important to her to have what pleasure she gets from smoking than to live a little longer. I empty the ashtray into my trash bag.

Gertie reaches out and suddenly puts her arm around me. "Bend down," she says, "I'll tell you a secret." When I don't bend down, she tells me anyway. "I think Yetta and Bernie are going to get married."

I just keep my face straight and don't answer. *Remember the rule, no talking to the old folks!*

Gertie says, "I'll tell you another secret, darling. Do you know why they're getting married? The young marry because they're hot, the old marry because they're cold. At night in bed, even the blankets don't do much good when you have old blood."

I pretend to take no notice and walk away. But her words stay with me. The old are cold. The young are hot. It's true! I think of Marcia in her red racing suit or in her pearly-white bikini, and I feel her heat—the heat of her youth, her energy, her need. Then I think of myself, always huddled in my jacket, even under the burning sun. I act like an old person, hunched and chilled. I wish I could be young. I deserve to be!

In the Game Room I put away someone's half-finished game of solitaire, sweeping up the cards and knocking them into a hard little pile. Then I put the marbles of the Chinese checkers game neatly on the dimples of the star painted on its tin base before I go down the hall to find my father. He's often somewhere in the basement, beyond the Game Room, checking the heating and cooling equipment, changing filters, lubricating various joints—whatever he does. I need to tell him about a shipment of pool chemicals that's coming in this afternoon—he has to be there to unlock the door of the Pool House for the delivery man.

As I pass the Storeroom, I hear a strange noise. It's a rubbing sound, as if someone is sanding wood. Simon? Who else could it be? And who gave him the key? So he's managed to get in there, illegally. First he manages to stay with his grandmother illegally, and now this! Nothing fazes those people. It's incredible!

I am about to knock loudly on the door when I hear another sound—a low shimmery laugh. Can it be...? It has to be! It can only be one person. There is no other possibility. It has to be Marcia! Marcia is in there with him. I don't believe this!

I want to run away but I stay. I stay; I stay and listen. The sound of sanding, the sound of Simon's low-pitched voice, then a whisper, then Marcia's silvery laugh. Not only have they met, but look how far they've gotten. Locked together in the Storeroom all alone, whispering and laughing.

I should go at once to find my father. *Tell him the pool chemicals are coming!* But I'm rooted to the spot as if my feet are hardened in cement. No one ever comes along this hall. I could stay here for an hour and listen and never be found out.

If only I could see them! If only there were portholes in the Storeroom wall, as there are in the pool. My heart is beating so hard it feels as if a bird is trapped in my chest, beating its wings against my crooked ribs; little crow inside big Crow.

But if I could see them the sight might burst my heart. Today they are talking and laughing, tomorrow kissing, the next day they will be entwined in each other's arms.

This is too much for me. I must find my father! I want to see him badly. Suddenly, I want to be near my father.

I comb the entire Sea 'n' Surf apartment complex looking for a door left ajar, the sign that my father is at work inside. When I get off the elevator on Gertie's floor, I see her door is open. Of all the places my father could be, he's here! I begin to wonder if some supernatural power is trying to mix me up in the lives of Gertie and her grandson.

"Dad?" I call.

"In here," he says. "In the bedroom."

"There was a call..." I say as I pass through Gertie's living room, where the fold-out couch is still open, and Simon's pajamas, blue with white seagulls on them, are tossed on top of the blanket. "The man from Aqua-Clear is coming with the pool chemicals at three this afternoon. He wants you to meet him to open the Pool House...."

My father is nowhere to be seen in the bedroom. I hear a muffled grunt.

"Where are you?"

"Under the bed," he murmurs.

"What are you doing *there*?"

"Wiring," he says. "Almost done..."

His feet come backing out first, and then he wriggles out like a big, wide worm. I don't usually have much interest in wires, but now he's holding a red button like a doorbell in his hand, and he's beginning to mark a place on the wall, just beside the bed, for screw holes.

"What's that?"

"Emergency alarm," he says.

"What for?"

"Mrs. Roth."

"I mean what *for*?"

"Bad heart. In case."

"In case of *what*?"

"In case she's dying," my father says. Methodically, he marks the screw holes, reaches for his drill, carefully drills. Then he brings up the wire from under the bed and connects it to the red doorbell. Then he screws the doorbell into the wall.

"Is Mrs. Roth dying?"

"We're all dying," my father says.

"Then why don't we all have alarm bells?" I ask him.

"We should," he says simply. He's all done. Now he's carrying his toolbox into the kitchen. I follow right behind him.

"What do you have to do in here?"

"Same thing." He's so laconic, so resigned. Nothing seems to make my father animated, excited. I watch him rummaging through things in his toolbox, which he's put on the stove. He's wearing blue jeans worn to faded softness and an old plaid shirt. His eyes are serious; he just does what he has to do.

"Is Mrs. Roth sicker than the other old people?"

"Her grandson says she's seriously ill."

"When did you talk to her grandson?"

"Yesterday—when I gave him the key."

"You gave him the key to the Storeroom?"

"Why not? He wants to make something in there, and we hardly use it for anything. It has that table in it he can use for a work bench...."

I realize there's no point debating this issue with him. He'll never see it my way. "What did he say about his grandmother?"

"He said she's got a very bad heart, that she's living on borrowed time. Mrs. Roth's daughter—that's the boy's mother, you know—asked the boy to see to it that I install these alarm buttons in the apartment, and then tell Mrs. Roth we're doing it in all the apartments, so she won't suspect they're worried about her."

"Where does the alarm ring?"

"Well, downstairs, at the switchboard, but also at the hospital. The hospital has a special service for old folks living alone—if they're in trouble, they're supposed to push the button. When the hospital gets the signal, they phone the apartment where the person lives. If the old person doesn't answer, they send out the paramedics and contact a family member."

"Sounds scary," I say. "I mean, Gertie looks fine to me."

My father is getting busy again, measuring, marking. He can't talk and work at the same time. I begin to wander around the apartment. I look again at the picture of the little family in the polished brass frame.

Young mother, young father, beautiful child. I look at Simon's pajamas with the gulls on them. He slept in them. He dreamed in them. His naked body was in them.

I feel I'm coming close to secrets that I shouldn't know. All around me are secrets—Gertie's secrets, Simon's secrets, my father's secrets, my...

There's a locked china cabinet against the wall, with some antiques in it. The key is in the lock. Beneath is a drawer with a keyhole. Very quietly (my father can't hear me, he's drilling in the kitchen) I take the key from the glass door and place it in the lock in the drawer and turn it. I slide open the drawer and see an old, leather picture album. Its surface is crumbling. I lift it carefully, kneel down on the floor and very slowly open it. Inside are many photographs of the same three people—I recognize them right away: the young woman alone, as a child, later, at perhaps thirteen, then at seventeen. In the wedding picture of the young woman and her handsome husband, she can't be even twenty. She's beautiful in all of them. Her eyes hold a special light, almost a sadness, though her smile is very sweet. Later, there's a picture of the baby in a pram and one on the knee of her father. There are also pictures of two older people—a stern-looking man in a high-collared suit, and a woman in a long, dark dress, heavy as tapestry, with white hair wound on top of her aristocratic head. In one picture she's carrying an umbrella, wearing high button shoes. If the young woman is Gertie, these must be Gertie's parents.

Could the baby in the pram be Simon's mother? Something compels me to carefully remove a photograph of the baby from the four little paper pockets, one at each corner of the picture, which hold it fastened into the album. I turn the picture over. My heart jumps. 1925 is written on the back in a spidery hand, in brown faded ink. If the baby were Simon's mother, she'd have to be over sixty now! It doesn't figure. If *my* mother were alive, she'd be only thirty-nine. My head is spinning from all this.

My father is calling me; he wants me to hold something for him as long as I'm here. I stuff the album back into the drawer and lock it, replacing the key in the china-cabinet door. Something about the pictures worries me—the dates don't work out. Something is wrong. A weird idea is beginning to exist at the back of my mind.

I go to help my father. I have no idea what wires I'm holding or why I'm holding them. I just hope I don't electrocute myself. Then again, maybe I hope I will.

Chapter Eight

I'm finally getting used to my haircut. For a while whenever I looked in the mirror, I could only think of Bernie's remark: "You look like one of those gorgeous poodles!" But as I walked along the beach this morning, I liked the way it looked in my shadow on the sand. The short curls blew in the breeze like a halo around my head.

I've been sitting here in the lifeguard station, on the splintery wooden seat, writing poetry most of the morning. I often come here. There hasn't been a lifeguard in this station for over a year. The city doesn't have enough money to man all the stations, so only the busiest beaches have lifeguards now. Once a little boy who was lost thought I was a lifeguard and asked me to help him find his mother. Luckily, she came running along the beach about five minutes later, looking for him. He was so sweet, gasping for breath as he sobbed, sitting on my lap, holding tight to my hand. I thought how wonderful it would be someday to have a child, to have the awesome responsibility for caring for another life.

But you need a man to share the job. And you need a man to start the baby. There are men up and down the beach. There are the joggers, determined men with their heads down and their elbows jaggedly stabbing the air; there are the bodybuilders, wide aggressive-looking men with muscles in their backs and thighs like curved mounds of flesh; and sometimes there are men who I guess are gay—their bodies seem delicate, somehow, their movement singular. Then there are just ordinary men, walkers on the beach, fathers, old men, teenage boys. But no men ever look at me.

Or if they do, they take me in and dismiss me. *What's that—that lump in a fat, blue jacket? Is it a girl or a thing? Whatever it is, it's of no interest.*

It's just me, the Crow, I want to tell them. Just a freak of nature. Just me, Faye, the *umglicklich feygl*.

There comes another one of them—males are all over the place. But this one looks familiar, coming down the beach with the wind billowing his shirt. His hair blazes in the sun.

I realize who it is, and I bend my head immediately, slouching down on the seat in the lifeguard stand. I pretend to be busy writing in my notebook. The poem I wrote is a mere column of words. I read up and down the page, and this is what I see:

LOVE
LOVE
LOVE
LOVE
LOVE
LOVE

That's how far gone I am. This is poetry? If it is, what is it really about? What does it mean?

The man is almost a man but not quite. It's Simon. He's coming right this way. He's holding a baby coconut in his hands, peeling the immature green layers away from the core. He tosses the peelings into the ocean. They rest on the wet sand till the bubbling foam of a wave creeps up and sweeps them into the sea.

He is just in front of me, walking by, wearing tennis shoes which seem to be filling up with sand. He stops just under my lifeguard stand and pulls off a shoe, shakes it out. Then he can't seem to put it on without losing his balance. When he tries to put it on, he has to hop to keep from falling.

"You can sit here to put your shoe on, if you want to."

I hear my voice and feel betrayed by it. I didn't mean to speak to him, I really didn't!

"Oh," he says looking up. "Hi! What are you doing up *there*? You're not a lifeguard, are you?"

Is he kidding? Does he really think they'd hire a crippled sixteen-year-old girl to be a lifeguard? But of course he doesn't know I'm crippled.

"I like to hang out here," I say. "No one bothers me."

My voice is not entirely friendly; why should it be? He's my adversary—he's living illegally in *my* building. Of course it's not my building—my father is merely an employee. It's more Marcia's building than mine—since her grandfather owns it.

"Can I come up there with you?"

"You can probably put on your shoe if you just lean against the side," I say.

"But I'd like to come up. See the view and all that."

I shrug. "Whatever...." I say. I carefully close my notebook and put it behind me on the bench. Simon comes climbing up the side with a couple of throws of his long legs.

He sits down beside me and starts brushing sand off his bare foot. I'm fascinated by his foot—how large and powerful it looks—the golden hairs on its arch, the long naked toes. I feel myself blushing.

He pulls off his other shoe and lets a shimmery waterfall of sand pour out.

"I love the climate here—it's so amazing after New York. I mean, to think that in December you can do this, while we're up there in a howling blizzard."

"It's very humid here sometimes," I say. I don't want him to think this is paradise. The next thing we know, he'll want to stay here with his grandmother for the winter!

"I'd love to live here," he says. "You're so lucky."

So there, I knew it. And how can he call me lucky! I'm the *unlucky* bird, not lucky at all.

"Is your grandmother very sick?" I have to get a straight answer and know the truth. I just haven't been able to believe that Gertie, with her peppy ways, her witty jokes, her wise sayings, is at death's door.

Simon looks down. "I'm afraid so," he says. "She's pretty bad, but of course she'd never admit it. How do you know?"

"My father told me about it. He was putting an alarm system into her apartment."

"Yeah—it's true. Your dad's a nice guy. He's letting me use the Storeroom to build a dulcimer."

"So I've heard," I say coldly. I don't tell him what else I heard, passing the Storeroom.

"How come the old folks call your father the Shadow?"

"Oh, do they?" I say. "And what do they call me?"

Simon keeps looking down. He can't meet my eyes. He shrugs. "I know your name is Faye. My grandmother told me. It's a pretty name."

"That's not what they call me," I say, looking off down the beach. "You must know that."

Simon stands up, it's been a short visit. I don't blame him. I haven't made it easy for him.

"Well, I'm glad no one is drowning," he says nervously. "I'm not such a hot swimmer. I'm going to practice, though."

I don't answer him.

"But I can't swim in the pool during the day with everyone looking. There are some terrific swimmers around—I get really embarrassed."

Terrific swimmers? Is he thinking of Yetta Korn? I definitely doubt it.

"You mean Marcia?" Why not pin him down?

He smiles at the mention of her name. His face reddens a little. "I'm going to start swimming at night," he confides. "When no one can see me."

At night! My time!

"You can't swim at night," I say. "The pool curfew is ten—that's when the pool closes. No one is allowed to swim at night."

"Oh well, rules," Simon says, with another foolish smile.

"There are reasons for rules," I say sternly.

"You could argue with my grandmother," Simon says. "She wouldn't be alive today if she had followed the rules."

"What do you mean?" I say, my heart skipping a beat.

"In the concentration camp," he says.

He looks at me, and I feel as if I'm losing my balance. I am teetering forward as if I'm going to topple right out of the lifeguard stand and land in the sand, headfirst.

"You're not kidding me?"

"I don't kid about that," he says. "Ever."

I feel as if I have no right to say anything, not one word. His words took the wind right out of my lungs.

"Do you want to know about it?" He sits back down on the splintery wooden seat. It seems as if he really wants to talk about it.

"Yes," I say.

"I don't know all that much," Simon says. He hits his fist against the wooden boards between us. "I mean, she doesn't like to talk about it; she starts to cry.

And then she says, 'At my age I have no time for tears. I owe it to my first family not to waste this life that only I was allowed to have on tears—I can cry later, when I'm dead. But I have to hurry and live for the ones who didn't live, so don't interrupt living, Simon.' That's what she says if I ask her to talk about it."

"Her *first* family?"

"That's what she calls them. We're her second family—my mother and the rest of us. Her first family was killed in camp. Her husband and her little girl."

"My God," I say.

I feel the ocean wind, see the sun sparkling on the whitecaps, see the ships on the horizon. I feel the life in me, feel myself alive as Simon says the words "killed in the camp." I even feel the hump of my back against the rough wooden boards of the lifeguard stand, and I'm grateful, suddenly, to be here. Hump and all.

"What do you know?" I ask Simon.

He shrugs. "You've heard that they let only the strong live, those who could work. And killed the babies. The children. They killed Gertie's daughter right away, she never told my mother exactly how, she can't talk about it. But my mother doesn't think the little girl was gassed; my mother thinks the SS soldiers just broke her head."

I am trying to match this news up with what I know of Gertie, the woman who kids around, who says little wise proverbs, who goes to exercise workouts, who plays canasta, who makes tea and serves *mandelbrot*.

"So..." Simon says. "After she lost her child, my grandmother got sick herself, couldn't eat even the rotten potatoes, the stale bread, whatever they gave her. So she was sent to the infirmary, where the sick were sent to die or to be experimented on. And when she got there, just as she was going in, a nurse who was coming out collapsed—she had typhus or whatever disease was going around—and this nurse just died, right in front of my grandmother. So Gertie changed clothes with her—in a freezing rain, my grandmother took off her rags, and put on the nurse's clothes and put the rags on the nurse's body, and went into the hospital, and pretended to be a nurse. And no one found out, and that's how she lived till the liberation."

"I have goose bumps all over me," I say. "Look." I hold out my arm to Simon, but of course he can't see the goose bumps, they're under my down jacket. Even in the sun, with the jacket on, I'm shivering.

Simon very gently moves the knitted cuff of my jacket up my arm a couple of inches, till he can see my skin. And the goose bumps.

"I know," he says. "It's unbelievable. So that's why Gertie doesn't worry too much about rules. The rules were that she was supposed to go into the hospital and die or be tortured to death, and breaking the rules meant she could live."

"She's such a cheerful woman," I say in amazement, amazed just thinking about it. "How can anyone who's suffered so much be so cheerful?"

"She'd say, if you asked her," Simon says, "that how could she *not* be cheerful, it's her job, her duty to those who can't be *any*thing."

Even Pretty Girls Cry at Night

Simon shakes his head, as if he hardly believes what he's just told me, and leans back in the lifeguard stand.

"You never know what people have to bear," he says. "You know?"

"I know," I say, thinking, at first, of myself. Then I think of my father and what he has to bear. And of my mother, who no longer bears anything. Then I remember what Gertie said about Marcia: "Even pretty girls cry at night." Maybe, though I doubt it. But maybe, just maybe... who could know?

"Well, I guess I should get back," Simon says. "I'm building this dulcimer," he says. "Your father, he's a nice guy, you know? To give me the key to the Storeroom."

I think, *Yes, you're in there against the rules,* but I don't say it. This isn't the moment to be sarcastic.

"Okay," I say, as Simon stands up, brushes the sand from his jeans and jumps down. "So long, then."

"See you soon," he says, and for that minute, I really believe he means it.

Chapter Nine

I'm a wonderful swimmer, maybe as good as Marcia—maybe even better. But I swim in the dark like a threatened octopus, and the darkness is my ink cloud, the screen which hides me. Tonight the stars are flickering as if there's heavenly overload; too many electric harps playing up there tonight. Maybe a heavenly party is going on, a celestial celebration.

I do water ballet in the starlight, pretending I'm Yetta Korn wearing a headful of cherries; I laugh to myself and jackknife to the bottom of the pool. This is when I have my fun, when I'm invisible, when I'm free.

I'm oddly lighthearted after talking to Simon this afternoon. I think he liked me! I felt he was interested! He's in my mind now like a neon man, electrified, buzzing. I keep thinking of the way he moved the knitted cuff of my jacket just an inch or two up my arm when I told him I had goose bumps. No man has ever touched me that way; gently, carefully. No man has ever *touched* me.

No wonder the story he told gave me goose bumps—what a terrifying story. And he told it so caringly, so sadly, as if he wanted to impress upon me how brave his grandmother was, how brave she still is. Maybe he came to see her this summer not because his parents were going to visit his aunt in Israel, but because he just wants to be with Gertie because she's so old... and so ill. Maybe he wants to get to know her while he still can.

But Gertie! Sick? Cheery, peppy Gertie? If it's true—and it must be true (why would anyone lie, why would my father have installed an alarm system if it weren't true?)—then things are not what they seem. Maybe *nothing* is what it seems.

I dive deep down into the swirling waters of this knotty thought. I skim the bottom of the pool with my eyes open. Even my own hands in front of me seem distorted. What if no one is who he seems to be? What if everything is distorted, unreal, make-believe?

Am I really the Crow, the mysterious, sulky, unlucky bird they call me? Maybe I'm the Fish, happy-go-lucky, cavorting like a dolphin, loving the feel of the water streaming off my face, along the underside of my hot body!

Or maybe I'm really a baby coconut, layers and layers of levels deep, the beginning of something great and strong and fine. Could my father not be what he seems, then? And Marcia? And her glamorous, sullen mother?

I scissors-kick from one end of the pool to the other, needing the movement, the release of energy. One of these nights, when I'm brave enough, I'll swim naked, just to see how it feels, just to know what it's like to have my body in the water without a single, separating thread of material.

I turn over and float on my back, arching skyward, toward the glimmering stars. There's no moon tonight, so I feel doubly concealed, doubly safe. I feel as if I'm right on the surface of the earth, arcing with the arc of the earth's curve, backbending for the long revolution around the sun. I could stay here all night and in the morning watch the sun's fire come through the clouds to warm me.

Fire! Explosion! The water turns red-orange all around me. Atomic attack! That's the first thought which flies through my mind at the bursts of light blasting forth at me from all sides of the pool! I am trapped in the brilliance—searchlights are coming straight at me. I have a sense of planes attacking, helicopters bearing down, beaming their merciless lights upon me. *What's happening?*

I kick wildly, flailing madly toward the side. Every underwater pool light is blazing, focused on me in the churning water! I see my legs kicking; I'm like an insect with a thousand legs. I can't move any of them fast enough.

Who turned on the pool lights? They're never on! Never! No one ever swims at night here! No one even knows about the lights. The switches are hidden in a fuse box in the Game Room; the fuse box is locked!

The thought occurs to me that someone is watching me! From below! I flail downward with all my strength till I can see through one of the portholes.

Like a scene in a nightmare, two laughing faces stare back at me. Marcia and Simon! Laughing! At me!

Beasts! Torturers! Monsters!

Do they think this is some funny little trick? I am bursting with fury! I kick up, climb out of the pool, run crazily for my jacket, dash away through the beach gate and flee across the sand toward the black, bottomless ocean.

I am going to drown myself. There is nothing else to do after they have made fun of me, looked at me as if I am a sideshow freak.

And all this after Simon and I had that long talk, after he came into my private lifeguard stand and sat with me, after he touched my arm! How could he do this to me?

I am already in the water, up to my waist, wading out to sea. My jacket, clutched in my arms, is soaked by the first gentle wave; already the down feathers are matting, bunching together, sucking water, going down like a drowning bird.

I can imagine my jacket washing up on shore after I'm drowned; a clotted mass of dark blue, dripping, heavy, useless. Heavy as lead, all its light warmth and comfort lost.

Then I imagine my father limping along the shore in the morning, searching for me and finding my jacket. I think about how he lost his buddy, Jim Ransome, about how he lost my mother, and finally, how—staring out at the blank ocean—he realizes he has lost me. He might want to wade in after me. He might not care what happens to him, might even want to die, too, and never again read *National Geographic* or wish that he lived in a stone cottage in Ireland.

I stop splashing toward the horizon. I won't do that to him. I have the choice not to do that to him. Gertie's little girl had no choice in the death camp; she couldn't spare her mother the pain of her death. But I have a choice. I can't do this to my father.

I wait the night out, huddled in a cabana, furious, humiliated, shamed, feeling murderous. I doze, wrapped in a big, dry towel, till the sun almost rises. I wait for the dim light that promises dawn. No one could possibly be at those portholes, staring into the pool which is still lit like a carnival. They have enjoyed their little joke and long ago gone to bed.

I make my way into the Game Room and see the open fuse box. Six switches are in the On position. I click them down, make sure the box is locked shut and finally go back to our apartment. The light glows into the hall from my father's partially open bedroom door, protecting him from the dark and from his fears.

I am grateful that he hasn't a new horror to wake to; I am grateful I had the good sense to save myself.

The next day Marcia and Simon are everywhere together. Playing checkers with each other, swimming together, walking on the beach together. Marcia seems proud. She links her arm in Simon's as they promenade along the pool deck, go through the gate to the beach. The old folks and I can hear them laughing as they chase each other across the sand, can hear her little screams as Simon throws baby coconuts at her.

Gertie and her friends are playing mah-jongg; I watch them set up the ivory tiles with mysterious jottings on them. Gertie talks to the women, and I hear the guttural sound in her voice; not the Bronx, but Poland. As I march around with my cleaning rag, my trash bag, I glance at Gertie and see the rows of gold bracelets on both her forearms. They jingle and tinkle like the clatter of wind chimes. I come closer and pretend to be cleaning a spot of ink from the folding table's top and I peer between the bracelets as her arms move—and yes! I see it! The number! Tattooed on her forearm. Her number from the concentration camp!

Gertie doesn't know what I'm looking at, but I'm so close to her that she reaches out and puts her hand on my arm. My down jacket buffers her touch. Nothing bad happened to it in the ocean. It's fine again, I put it in the dryer with a clean tennis shoe, and the shoe beat the feathers apart as they dried. My jacket is as good as new now. But what does she want? The other women are watching her.

"It's not permanent," is what she whispers to me. What does she mean? She says it again. "Don't worry, darling. It's not permanent."

I gently withdraw my arm and walk away as if I heard nothing. She knows I don't speak to any of them; she can't expect me to change now. Besides, I have no idea what she's talking about.

I see my father kneeling at the far end of the pool, testing the chemical balance. He tests for pH level, for acid level. He adds chlorine; he adds powders and potions and lotions and algicides.

When he sees me, he says, "Did you open the Pool House?"

"No," I answer.

"It was open," he says. "I'm very careful, with those dangerous chemicals in there. I know I didn't leave it open."

I shrug. He isn't accusing me; he knows I'm careful, too. I consider telling him that the fuse box was open as well, but I don't, because then I'd have to tell him about the lights in the pool and how I was swimming after dark. He doesn't know I swim at night. No one knows. Or no one knew, till *they* did that to me. But how did they get into the Pool House? And the next question, the logical follow-up: why were they in there and what were they doing?

I don't want to know. No. I can't bear to think about that!

But all night I think about it. Sex and what it must be like to be together with a man in a dark, private place like the Pool House. I can imagine the darkness, the heat, the whispers; I can feel the sense of secrecy and wildness which would charge the air. If the touch of Simon's fingers on my arm is still alive and electric in me, what would it be like to have him embrace me, press himself against me, kiss me?

But then I see his laughing face in the porthole and I'm humiliated again. Let him make love to Marcia in the Pool House, let them fall into a vat of acid! Let the diatoms creep out of the metal tub and devour the two of them. Or at least Marcia. Simon I'd still like to confront—I have a matter to settle with him.

Chapter Ten

Two days later I get the shock of my life when—with my notebook under my arm—I go down the beach to the lifeguard station and see that someone is in it. Not some*one*, but two: a couple! I think at first it's just some couple, any couple, a boy and a girl from anywhere, but as I get closer I realize the couple is not a pair of strangers at all—it's Simon and Marcia.

My fury, which has been simmering since they exposed me in the pool, returns in a blazing flare. I know, I know—I don't own the pool, I don't own the beach, I don't own the world, but certain things have become mine by means of my connection to them, by time spent, by closeness. When I stare at the ocean long enough, I begin to believe it belongs to me. I've spent a thousand hours there; I've thought all my crazy, sad, wild thoughts there, and that's where I've written a notebook full of my poems. Most important of all—I sat there with Simon. That's what kills me. Simon sitting with me in the lifeguard stand: that's the image I've thought about over and over; how I sat there with Simon, and talked to him about scary, private matters, and he touched my arm. For one instant he touched my arm, and I've thought about that touch over and over. Perhaps it's the most important thing that ever happened to me.

Now the pair of them have taken over everything. My whole world—they've just filled it up with their smug laughter, their cocky togetherness, and they've shut me out. No place is mine, there's nowhere to hide anymore. The two of them are everywhere. They turn up in the Game Room, the hallways, the lobby, the Exercise Room. They lock themselves in the Storeroom where they secretly do God-knows-what. And now they're in my lifeguard stand!

I don't want to let them see me. I'm afraid of their seeing me and imagining how pathetic I am. When there's two against one, the one alone is always pathetic. I turn my back and run away over the sand; my heels sink in as they hit the little hills of soft sand. I wish the beach were made of quicksand and all of me could sink in and disappear forever.

I stare down at my feet and see my toes; I never realized before how ridiculous toes are—funny, short appendages, flipping along, with little nails on them. The toes are all a different size. They're bizarre.

I begin to think of how ridiculous other human parts are—head, with all those queer holes in them. Holes for seeing out of, holes for breathing air, holes for hearing, a great big hole for stuffing food in. We're all monstrous, I think, as weird as any alien from outer space might be.

This thought makes me feel better. Marcia, with her beautiful body and golden hair, is just another weird creature with little irregular toes and a head full of holes and pairs of flapping arms and legs that fold in the middle. Simon is even more ridiculous because he's a man and has his manly parts—those strange appendages which hang peculiarly and threateningly on the outside of his body.

They're both freaks. Good! I'm glad of it. I'm not the only weird one around. We're all deformed in our own ways. Yes, indeed, compared with the seashells on the shore—shining, white, balanced, gracefully designed—we humans are just an accident of nature.

I am rushing along so fast I almost trip on a body. A pair of thin, tanned legs is sticking off a blanket, toes up. These toes have painted toenails; a hue of purple. How foolish: to try to hide the hideousness of toes by painting the edges of them ridiculous, unnatural colors!

The body looks unconscious...or dead. It's a woman: I can tell at once from the shape inside her elegant-looking bathing suit. The mouth is partially open; the holes of the eyes are covered by huge, mirrored sunglasses. The nose...

I know this body. This is Marcia's mother, Florence King. I have never been so close to the woman before, and what I see shocks me. She looks old, not glamorous at all. Her suntan isn't healthy looking; her skin is so darkly yellow-brown that she looks jaundiced. And she's so thin, sickly thin. I used to think she was thin like a model, but at this close range she looks undernourished and sick. The way her mouth hangs open, slack, gives her the look of a very old person. I feel as if I ought to cover her face with a corner of her towel, to protect her privacy.

I try to reconcile this form with the woman I have admired and envied from a distance. Usually, she's wearing her designer clothes and her high heels, and she looks very determined and tough. She's often just leaving the apartment building when I see her, on her way to the stores with Marcia, and at those times she looks sinewy, cool, with a soft leather purse tossed over her shoulder. But here she looks helpless and sick. She doesn't seem to be sunbathing, or even sleeping; she looks almost unconscious.

I wonder if Marcia knows she's here. I glance back and see her head and Simon's head close together in the lifeguard stand. Marcia isn't thinking about her mother at this moment, I am certain of that.

The woman groans.

I go over to her and say, "Mrs. King, are you all right?"

She sits up suddenly, propping herself on her elbow. She says nothing, but her eyes seem astonished. Then she turns her head to the side and throws up into the sand.

"Are you very sick?" I say, feeling frightened.

She waves me away and vomits again. When she raises her head, she says, without looking at me, "Please go away."

"But can I help you? Do you want to go home? I could call a doctor."

She shakes her head so slowly, so sadly, it's as if she is saying there's no use, no doctor can help her. She motions with her hand for me to go away.

So I go.

Maybe it's flu, I think. But I know it isn't flu. I don't know what it is, but I know it's bad. I know it's much worse than flu.

And then I think of Marcia, just down the beach, her body pressed against Simon's, doing the one thing in the world I most want to do, and I think how I've always imagined that Marcia has the perfect life.

But where, in her perfect life, does this sick mother fit in? Where in a perfect life can you fit in a beautiful woman with a face full of sorrow and shame?

I feel a shock of cold water against my ankles and realize the tide has come up. As the wave recedes it leaves a tangle of black seaweed wrapped around my legs. I try to shake it off, but the strands cling to me like live creatures.

Even after I peel off the seaweed and run back home, I can still feel the imprint of the cold, slimy threads flapping against my skin.

At dinnertime, when my father is eating hot dogs and beans I made for us, I ask him if anything is wrong with Florence King.

"What makes you ask?" my father says. I'm surprised at his quick attention to me; usually he reads his magazine for ten minutes before he even realizes I've asked him anything.

"I saw her on the beach today. She looks sick."

"It's not our business," my father says.

"Maybe she needs a doctor."

"She knows where to find one," he says. Then he goes back to reading. This time he's reading *Organic Gardening*. It comes once a month, and sometimes after he reads it he talks about moving to the hills of Georgia and growing his own food.

But this conversation is clearly over. You don't get my father to talk when he doesn't want to say anything. If I've learned anything in all these years, I've learned that.

I have a sudden desire to ask Gertie if she knows what's wrong with Florence King. Maybe she has cancer, I think with sudden shock. If that's true, then Marcia might lose her mother just as I did.

Surely Gertie would know the truth. Gertie knows everything. And I'm sure she'd tell me all she knows if I gave her a chance. But I can't ask her! It's my policy. I never talk to the old folks.

I begin to wish I could break my own rule. Gertie knows so much, she's lived through so much, she could teach me how to deal with the hard, terrible things in my life, she could help me figure things out. But I'm locked into my own little cage by my own little rule.

Why don't I break the rule? Gertie believes in breaking rules. Sometimes rules don't apply. Sometimes rules can be fatal.

My father holds out his cup and looks at me apologetically; he'd like me to get him more coffee. His bad leg always hurts more at the end of the day, and he'd rather not stand up to get it for himself. I refill his cup from the coffee maker, and he thanks me. He always thanks me. He's a kind man. At least I have that to be thankful for.

Cancer. If Florence King has cancer she is not lucky. If Marcia's mother is dying of cancer, am I still entitled to consider Marcia lucky?

I add up my bad luck: my deformed back, my mother's dying young, my father's lameness, my father's sadness. What sum does that come to? Is there a number to which this all adds up? If Marcia did her arithmetic, what answer would she get? A beautiful face, a beautiful body, divorced parents, a very sick mother.

Does she come out ahead of me? The fact that she has Simon mad about her convinces me she does. She gets a better grade on the test. But it's a peculiar form of mathematics; it makes me deeply uncomfortable to be doing this sort of homework.

Chapter Eleven

What's this? Marcia on the high dive with a magnificent young man who is tall, muscular, black-haired! He looks exactly like the diver who won the gold medal during the Olympics in Los Angeles. I can't believe my eyes. Three weeks of seeing Marcia sticking to Simon as if she were his Siamese twin, and now she's here smiling up at this exquisite man as if she's hypnotized.

Don't have a fit, I tell myself. *Don't jump to any conclusions.* Calmly, I go about my chores, straightening the lounge chairs, sweeping up the little paper rings that Bernie flicks off his cigars, gathering damp, sandy towels. Now and then I glance up at the high dive; Marcia seems to be getting lessons. Mr. Olympics takes a position on the high dive. He places his heels over the edge, his back to the pool. He demonstrates the exact position of the heels, just so. Then, taking her by the shoulders, he moves her behind him. They change places, moving very carefully up there, so high above the rest of us. She wiggles her heels into place.

"Perfect," the young man says as if he's speaking to every one of us. His voice is deep, resonant. He's much more of a man than Simon. He's at least twenty-five. Marcia is clearly impressed. But then, who wouldn't be? This is an impressive man.

"I should only be eighteen again," says Yetta Korn, coming along the pool deck in her high-heeled cloppers. She shades her eyes and looks up. "I would be up there myself. But frankly," she whispers, coming close to me, "I think my Bernie has better legs. Don't you agree?" When I don't answer her she explains the mystery of her perception to both of us: "But I'm in love, darling. Like the song says, 'I'm in love with a wonderful guy!'"

The thought of anyone being in love with Bernie Kriegel makes me smile involuntarily.

"You approve!" Yetta Korn says to me. "That's because you understand, like the wise girl you are, that at any age love is wonderful. Wait, some day it will come to you, *Feygele*. But don't be in too much of a hurry. You have time, believe me. Life is long."

Yetta dips her head, and the cherries on her bathing cap rattle gaily. "Oh here comes my lover-boy," she says. "Just the sight of him gives me high blood pressure. At my age, I suppose this could be dangerous."

Bernie comes out toward the pool wearing a terry-cloth beach robe, smoking his eternal cigar, carrying the *Wall Street Journal* under his arm.

"Yoo-hoo, Handsome," Yetta Korn calls to him.

"Hello, Sweet-lips," Bernie says. "You're a sight for sore eyes."

"You haven't seen anything, yet. Watch this, Angel, I'm going to do this just for you," Yetta says and kicks off her clogs and jumps like a hippo into the pool.

The wake of Yetta's leap causes water to slosh madly against the sides of the pool.

"A graceful woman," Bernie says to me. I don't know if he's kidding or if he's really blinded by love.

I look up at Marcia, expecting to see her usual look of annoyance and irritation which comes over her face when she has Yetta to deal with. But her gaze is transfixed by Mr. Olympics; she's out of it totally.

Bernie has opened his newspaper. Immediately a small smile appears on his face. He glances up and sees me looking at him. "I have a winner," he confides in me. "I bought five hundred shares of Galaxy yesterday, and it's up three points today."

Galaxy. I wonder if they're selling shares in the planets and stars now.

"Bernie, come in the water. It's like a bathtub."

"If I wanted to take a bath, I'd go upstairs and climb into my bathtub," he says.

"Swimming is good for your circulation," Yetta says enticingly.

"Not as good for me as your massages," Bernie says, and looking at me, he winks. I hurry away with my towels. Just as I approach the steps to the Game

Room, Gertie emerges holding onto Simon's arm. She's looking very pale, walking slowly.

"Good morning, *Feygele*," she says to me. "I'm a little under the weather, so it's good to have a strong arm to lean on." Simon looks embarrassed to be confronted by me. He looks beyond my head, and I see him take in the scene at once. The high dive. Marcia. The gorgeous hunk.

He pulls back his head like a turtle who has peeked out of his shell and finds it dangerous.

"I forgot something upstairs," he mumbles.

"Just walk me to a chair, darling," Gertie asks him. But he's already let go of her. He wants to disappear. His desperation is evident. He backs away, and Gertie, suddenly unbalanced, reaches for my arm. I can't shake her off; she would fall, so I let her lean on me while Simon runs away. Gertie sees the scene on the diving board, too; she's no dummy.

"So," she says. "A new diversion for the Beauty."

I'm stranded, stuck, with Gertie Roth hanging on to my arm.

"It had to be," she says. "You and I both knew that girl couldn't be satisfied with one boy for long. She needs attention from men like her mother needs drugs and drink."

I stare at Gertie, but she isn't looking at me, she's just taking slow steps toward a lounge chair. Her bracelets slide upon one another, making a dull jangle. Even when she's wearing a bathing suit, as she is now, she puts on her gold bangles. I wonder if she sleeps in her bracelets. Maybe she doesn't ever want to see that number engraved in blue ink in the skin of her arm.

"Right here, this beach chair will be fine. Thank you, darling." I disentangle my arm from hers and stand there till she's safely stretched out on the lounge. The Canasta Ladies come out, too, and wave to Gertie. They proceed to set up a game at their little table.

"Count me out," Gertie calls to them. "I'm tired today. For some reason, I didn't sleep too good last night."

"Too much riding on the exercise bike," one of them calls back. "I told you, at your age, you shouldn't do so many miles."

"If I don't do them at my age," Gertie says, "when will I do them?" She laughs, but then a shock passes over her face and she puts her hand to her chest. An instant later she looks up and says, "It's nothing. A skipped beat. It's going fine again. Sometimes now and then I think my heart stops for a second, but my doctor says that's my imagination."

Now I am afraid to leave her. Sometimes she thinks her heart stops!

"My grandson has gone upstairs because he's shamed," she says to me softly. "Too bad you can't play a game of checkers with him. If he could only get to know you, darling, he'd see what real quality is."

Then Gertie gasps, and I think her heart has stopped. But she motions to the pool where Mr. Olympics is in midair, doing a triple flip. He enters the water like an arrow. Perfect. When he surfaces everyone applauds.

"Now you try it, hon," he calls up to Marcia, shaking his head as if he's a wet dog. Water flies from his hair in sparkling drops.

"Me do that?" she calls down charmingly. How coy she is. And of course he has to coax her.

"You know you can do it. You're top-notch. Just put your mind where it's at."

"My little mind?" she calls down from the high dive, and I think bitterly, *Yes, Marcia, your little mind!*

So Marcia takes her stand. She steps forward. She wiggles her toes. She wiggles her hips. She wiggles her shoulders. She extends her arms up toward the sun like a queen about to bless her people. Then she turns around and positions her heels. She waits. All at once she leaps up, taking strength from a source deep in her powerful calves. She somersaults and twists on her way down and cuts into the deep blue water of the pool. I find I am holding my breath till she rises up like a bobbing toy. When she clears the water from her eyes, she swims forward into the arms of the beautiful man.

He hugs her. She laughs. Standing chest high in the water, he hugs her again. The old people applaud: a fairy-tale romance is taking place right before their tired old eyes.

And then I glance up at the window of Gertie's apartment. I see Simon staring out. He's standing stiff as a rod. His body seems as hollow as a scarecrow's. He's frozen there, studying the tableau.

I feel a hand on my thigh; it's sharp, like the claw of a bird. Gertie is pushing me away from her chair.

"Go to him," she says. "Go up there. He needs you. What can you lose?"

Chapter Twelve

I don't go. Gertie doesn't understand how raw Simon's hurt is; how shamed he must feel. Or maybe she understands, but thinks I can make it better by kissing the hurt. I'm not into kissing. She ought to know that.

His hurt may even be my triumph, but it's too soon for me to feel any satisfaction. And I don't hang around to see the second act. I go back to my room where I take my mother's old, battered guitar off the wall and play "Mary Hamilton," a song my father once told me she used to love. I taught myself to play the guitar. I'm pretty bad at it, but I love the sound the strings make. I have all my mother's old Joan Baez albums. Sometimes I play along with the songs and try to understand what my mother must have felt like when she was a young woman. "Mary Hamilton" is about a woman who gets pregnant by a king, and then the king has her beheaded. I suppose men have used women badly since the beginning of time; somehow, I feel a certain sympathy for the way Marcia is treating Simon. Not that he's a bad person; he's just a man, and men don't always see women for what they really are. So many men judge women immediately by the way they look. It's the simplest arithmetic in the world; a man counts up the pretty parts of a woman, and the higher the score the more the man wants to be seen with her. And Marcia, God knows, has a great number of pretty parts. And knows how to use them. But maybe she resents having to use those parts. I know *I* would resent it. It's something I never thought about before. That being a beautiful woman might be a problem, that beauty might attract men for the wrong reasons.

Well, I have better things to worry about. I'll never in my life have to concern myself with *that*.

I am doing my father's laundry in one of the basement washers late at night. It's my swimming time, but the joy has gone out of it for me after being caught in the pool that night in the blaze of spotlights the conspirators trained on me. I like it here in the Laundry Room, with the sweet scent of detergent, the pungent scent of bleach all around me. Someone else has set his clothes to washing. Mine are already in the dryer. The clothes tumble and spin in the hot, metal drum: my father's plaid shirts, his blue jeans, his underwear, his socks. And my few things. What do I wear besides this fluff of feathers? Things that don't show—it hardly matters what.

I have the briefest fantasy of how nice it would be to care about clothes—to choose the ones that are prettiest, look the nicest, clothes that suit one's very soul. But there I go, coming right back to the subject of beauty. Best to think about other things.

I feel lulled by the thump and thud of the clothes spinning round. I could almost fall asleep here. It's warm and private. It's like a little dim cement tomb. Except that someone is doubtless going to come in and put his clothes in one of the dryers in a few minutes. Except that I am aware of noises coming from the Storeroom. Plunks and thuds and loud buzzes from a drill. Simon building his dulcimer. Let him drill till kingdom come. Who cares what he does? He'll be twanging away all alone for the rest of the summer, from the looks of things. Tonight I saw Marcia, dressed to the teeth, going out on the arm of Mr. Olympics. She was wearing a delicate pink sundress, with tiny ribbon straps that tied in bows over her sunburned, powerful shoulders. She had a furry, white sweater over her arm. Where were they going? Dinner? The movies? To sit on a bench at the beach from which they would watch the moon over the ocean?

That's only fair, isn't it? Marcia watches the moon over the ocean, and I watch my father's clothes revolve in the clothes dryer.

I sense a burning just under my eyes and recognize the warning of tears. Luckily I stop them in time; someone is coming down the hall.

I pretend to be reading *Organic Gardening*. I always take a magazine down into the Laundry Room, just in case I have to avoid conversation with someone who wanders in.

Florence King comes in and looks right at me. She doesn't recognize me. She looks at me, looks *through* me as if I didn't exist, as if she never saw me in her life. She's wearing a long, blue, shimmery robe with ruffles at the hem and neckline. It looks very expensive, except that it has brown stains on it, as if she'd spilled her cup of coffee in her lap. I wonder why, if she's washing clothes, she didn't think to wash her robe. It sure could use washing.

I feel her staring at me. I wonder if she's remembering that time on the beach when she was so sick on the sand. But she's staring at me as if she can't remember where she is or what she's doing here in the Laundry Room. I begin to feel very weird. I get up and open my dryer and poke around inside it, as if I'm seeing if my clothes are dry. That seems to give her a hint of what to do here. She starts opening the tops of empty washing machines, looking for her clothes. When she gets to the one which is in the spin cycle, she leans against it so that her entire body vibrates with the vibration of the machine.

Can she be sleepwalking with her eyes open? She has the blankest expression on her face I've ever seen. Her hair is wild, as if she hasn't combed it all day. When the machine stops spinning, it clunks to a halt and jars her to attention. She tries to open the lid, but it's not the lid she's pulling on, it's the handle of the lint trap. It comes out of the machine, a long, rectangular strainer, and she stands there with it in her hand, baffled.

"Would you?" she says to me, stumbling slightly.

I put down my magazine and go over to take the lint trap from her hand and replace it in the machine. I open the lid and begin to pull out her clothes from the washer and toss them into an empty dryer.

"Good," she says. "I can't manage that now."

I am doing this for her because she's the daughter of the owner, and my father needs his job to support us. I'm not doing it to be kind. I don't feel kind tonight. If this woman had never had a child, then Marcia wouldn't be living here under my nose day and night, wouldn't have taken and then discarded Simon, wouldn't be sitting right now on a bench at the beach with a beautiful young man beside her as they watch the moon climb over the ocean.

"Good," she says again, and lurches toward the door. "In the morning," she mumbles. "I'll try to come back in the morning."

Chapter Thirteen

The next morning the front desk buzzes me to say that a carpet truck is here with the new carpet for the front lobby. My father has to sign the invoice before they begin to install it.

But where is my father? I tell the woman at the desk I will try to find him. I feel a tremendous irritation at being interrupted. Not that I'm doing anything so special; I'm just lying on my bed, thinking. But thinking is important to me. It entertains me, interests me. And now I have to start walking through the entire building, floor by floor. It could take me an hour to find him.

I begin on the second floor; no open doors. The third floor. No open doors. The fourth floor. Ah, thank God. I see a door that's slightly open. My father has got to be in there—the old people never leave their doors open. They're very nervous and suspicious. Some of them have special peepholes and double bolts and queer little locking knobs that fit over their doorknobs.

Aha—it's Bernie Kriegel's apartment he's working in. I wonder what went wrong there. Bernie's apartment is full of amazing appliances—he has so much money he buys every new contraption that comes out. He has a computer, a video recorder, a microwave oven (which he never uses), a ham radio, a TV with a giant screen. I know all this because Yetta Korn brags to the Canasta Ladies about how rich he is, how he's rolling in money.

"Dad?" I call, pushing the door of Bernie's apartment open a little further. "It's me."

There's silence inside.

"Dad? Are you there?"

I walk into the apartment. I hear a tiny rustling sound. Maybe he's under the bed or has his head inside a kitchen cabinet and can't hear me. I walk into the bedroom, saying loudly, "It's Faye, Dad. Where are you?"

"Don't tell on me!" cries a voice. "Oh please don't tell!"

I spin around! And there's Marcia! She's standing in Bernie's closet. She has her hand in the pocket of one of his jackets.

What am I supposed to say to her? *Hi, how are you? What are you doing in Bernie's closet? How was your date last night?* So I don't say anything, but just stand there.

Finally she comes out of the closet. She doesn't look like a hibiscus flower right now; she looks pale, scared, terrified. I realize I've never seen her before without a smug look on her face. She looks like an entirely different person.

Suddenly she sinks down on Bernie's bed and begins to cry. "Oh please, I beg you, Crow, don't tell."

"My name isn't Crow," I say. "It's Faye."

"I'm not here for the reason you think," she says.

"I'm not thinking anything. Were you collecting Bernie's jackets to be dry-cleaned?" I suggest. I'm really just trying to explain this situation to myself.

"I didn't take anything!" she says. She holds out her hands, palms up. "See? I thought he would have money around, he's so rich. But he doesn't have a single dollar bill anywhere."

"Of course not," I say. "Rich people don't bother with cash."

"I was desperate," Marcia says.

I sit down on the bed, too. My knees are feeling weak. Why is she desperate? Is she pregnant? Did Mr. Olympics work that fast? Or was it Simon? No, I decide. Simon is too serious for that. He'd have used birth control.

"Did Simon make you pregnant?" I say, just to be sure.

"Simon!" She laughs oddly. "He's only a child. He probably won't go that far till his wedding night."

"Oh," I say. I have to reconstruct all my thoughts around that idea now.

"Then who did?"

"Who did what?"

"Made you pregnant?"

"I'm not pregnant," she says. "Oh God, maybe I wish I were. It would be easier than this."

"Than what?"

"Easier than my mother being a coke head."

"What do you mean?"

"Were you born yesterday, Crow?"

"I asked you not to call me Crow. Unless you want me to call you Beauty."

"Some Beauty I am," Marcia says. "I feel more like the Beast."

We both hear a noise in the hall. She jumps up, then runs to the window. "It's okay," she says. "Bernie is still out there by the pool. He's usually there all morning. That's why I came up here, as soon as I knew he was outside."

"But why are you in here, Marcia?" I ask. I hear a certain authority in my voice. Because of my father's job, I feel a responsibility to the tenants of the Sea 'n' Surf.

"I needed some money for my mother," Marcia whispers. "She's going nuts. She needs her drugs or she gets sick. And I can't stand to see her that sick."

"Sick people need to see a doctor, not take what only makes them sicker."

"Try to tell her that," Marcia says.

"I saw her in the Laundry Room last night," I say. "She could hardly figure out which machine her clothes were in."

"She was drunk," Marcia says. "When she can't get cocaine she just drinks twice as much. And when

I'm not there with her, she gets worse. Last night I was out till late."

"So I imagined," I say.

"So you can see I'm not a thief," Marcia begs me. "I just needed some money till my mother can get some more cash from my grandfather. He used to be very generous to us, but lately my mother is asking for so much, I think he's getting suspicious."

"I think we ought to get out of here," I say, "and talk about this someplace else."

"Do you have some money to lend me?" Marcia asks.

"I don't think that's what we ought to talk about," I say. "I think you have to consider some other solution."

"*Would* you talk to me?" Marcia asks. "I mean, I've always wished we could talk, that we could be friends. I mean, we're the same age and all that, and everyone else here is a hundred years old. But you always seem so snobbish."

"Snobbish?"

"Yes," Marcia says. "Like you're too good to be with anyone else."

"Or too bad," I say.

She goes to Bernie's closet and closes the door. "I'm glad he didn't have any money in his pockets," she says. "I knew that once I started stealing for my mother, I would never be the same."

"How did you get in here?" I ask.

"I can't tell," Marcia says suddenly.

"You have to tell," I say. "I want to know. This is a high-security building."

"Well, so what if you know? I got the key from Simon," Marcia says. "I made him give it to me when he had the master key to open the Storeroom. I had a copy of it made."

"My God!" I say. "So that's how the two of you opened the fuse box in the Game Room."

"It wasn't his idea. It was mine," Marcia says. "I'm sorry."

"You're sorry?"

"For shining the lights on you that night."

"You should be sorry," I say. "You really should be." I start pushing Marcia toward the door, gently. "Let's get out of here now."

"Where can we go?"

"I think you should go back to your apartment now. I have to find my father—there's a rug delivery truck waiting downstairs. But I'll meet you down by the cabanas in twenty minutes. Then we can walk on the beach and talk about this."

"Twenty minutes?" She looks very worried.

"Fifteen then."

Chapter Fourteen

When I come down to the cabanas Marcia is nowhere in sight. It took me more than fifteen minutes to find my father. Just my luck—he happened to be on the eleventh floor, replacing the rusted-out faucets in one of the vacant apartments. I had to comb each floor, door by door. I decide we ought to have a better system in the future; he ought to get a beeper, to be paged like a doctor.

But where would Marcia have gone? I scan the pool area. Bernie and Yetta are on adjacent beach chairs, holding hands. His face is covered by his newspaper, and her face is covered by *Bride's* magazine, open at the center. One of the Canasta Ladies is standing in the shallow end of the pool, holding a Styrofoam cup, which she keeps filling and dumping down the front of her bathing suit.

She looks up and sees me watching her.

"I know it's easier if you go in all at once," she says to me, smiling. "But I'm a coward."

I'd like to ask her if she's seen Marcia, but I'm restricted by my rule. I really want to say something to her. I'm tired of my self-imposed silence. Why, exactly, do I refuse to talk to the old folks? I don't quite remember the reasons for my rule; the rule is just beginning to seem a little pointless to me. The old people are real people. They have things to say to me. And sometimes I have things to say to them. But I'm stuck now—once you make a rule, you're obliged to stick to it even if it no longer applies. At least you stick to it if you're stubborn like me.

I go in and out of the cabanas, fast, as if I'm working, checking up on wet towels, used glasses. She's not there. I look out past the pool gate to the beach, but I don't see her. Could she be in the lifeguard station?

Just as I am about to walk out to the sandy beach, I notice something funny about the Pool House. It's not that the door is open—it isn't—but the silver handle is tilted down instead of pointing straight out. A little alarm goes off in my head. If the latch were clicked properly, the handle would be horizontal. I didn't even know I knew this, but I do.

I go over and push on the door. It opens easily. A strong smell of chlorine practically overpowers me. The fumes sting my eyes and make me cough. It's dark in the Pool House, but I can see Marcia's feet in a little beam of light coming in from a screened vent near the floor.

"What are you doing in here?"

"There's nothing you can do," Marcia says. "I've already taken it."

"Taken what?" I open the door wider in order to see her better. She's standing in the back of the Pool House beside the open drum of chlorine.

"Poison," Marcia says. She hits the drum. "At least that's what it says."

I know what it says. On the white plastic surface is the emblem of a skull and crossbones. "Danger!" is what the big red letters say. "Corrosive. May be fatal if swallowed." This stuff is no joke. Even my father wears gloves when he's handling it.

"How much did you take?"

She shrugs. "Enough, I hope."

Now I can see that she's holding a cup in her hand, filled with some liquid.

"Come with me," I say, taking the cup. With my other hand I grab Marcia's arm. She doesn't resist—it's as if she's given up all her problems into my care. She just follows along as I drag her, careful not to spill the contents of the cup, past the staring old folks at the pool, through the lobby where the new carpet is being laid, out to Collins Avenue, where I hail a cab.

"Mt. Sinai Hospital," I say. "Emergency room."

"We're going to keep her under observation," a nurse tells me when she comes into the waiting room after what seems like a very long time. "We don't think she swallowed very much; from what she told us, it tasted too bad."

"Can I talk to her?"

"I don't see why not," the nurse says. "She's bound to be here for a few hours. And can you help us get in touch with her parents? She's very agitated. We want to see that she gets some help."

"I know where you can reach her mother," I say. "But it's really her mother who needs the help."

"What do you mean?"

"It's complicated," I say.

"Well, tell us what you can," the nurse says. "We'll be grateful. The doctor will want to know all you can tell us."

"I've blown my life to kingdom come," Marcia says when I come into the partitioned cubicle where she's resting. She's in a blue hospital gown and looks very childlike. "There's no going back now."

"This is the best thing," I say. "Now maybe your mother can get some help. And you, too."

"She'll be furious," Marcia says. "She doesn't think she needs help. She tells me she can stop taking drugs whenever she wants to, that she only takes the stuff because she's in a hard place in her life."

"Who isn't?" I say. "Who isn't in a hard place...?"

"You're not," Marcia says.

"Me? Why do you say that?"

"You have it all together," Marcia says. "You always seem so independent. Never needing anyone."

"Me independent? I always thought you were the independent one," I say.

"I've always wondered how you do it; how you ignore the old people and don't get angry at their chatter and gossip. And how you seem to like being alone—you take long walks on the beach, you do your job. You're always so serene. As if you don't need anything. But me—I always feel I must have something. I think that if I get something I don't have I'll feel better. And then, even if I get it—new clothes or some new guy liking me—it doesn't seem to help. Then I need something else."

"Isn't your swimming important to you?"

"I guess it is," Marcia says. "Yes—it really is. But it's not enough."

"What would be enough. What do you think would make you happy?"

Marcia laughs. "Don't laugh," she says. "Being you for a day, figuring out how you handle all the bad stuff."

I can't believe this conversation is happening here, in this room, between Marcia and me.

"I really wish I knew why you wear this weird jacket of yours all the time." She reaches her hand out and gently pinches some of the feathers in my jacket sleeve between her fingers. "Why on earth do you?"

"It's a long story," I say.

"Does it have to do with your father? I mean, I thought maybe he's possessive of you or something, and doesn't want you to show your body."

"Oh, no," I say. "My father has nothing to do with this, believe me. He's the nicest man in the world."

"I wish I could say that about *my* father. He's terrible, a terrible man. You wouldn't believe what he tried to do to me when I was younger."

"You're not saying he...?"

"Well, yes, I am. At least he tried. They say it's very common, that kind of thing. Luckily I had the sense to tell my mother, and she made him leave."

"My God!" I say. "I had this whole picture in my mind about you and the kind of life you lead, and it's all crashing to pieces now."

"Life is one big crash," Marcia said. "Isn't it?"

When Florence King came into the room, she began to cry. Marcia sat up in bed and said, "I'm really all right, Mommy," and she also began to cry. When they started hugging each other, I left quietly. The way Marcia had said "Mommy" made me feel sadder than almost anything in my life.

Chapter Fifteen

Plunk! Plunk! Plunk! Sad, dull sounds coming from the Storeroom. That's what Simon must be doing these days, sitting by himself in that dim little room, plunking on the strings of his dulcimer. Well, good for him. Whenever I think about him a hot flash of anger zips across my chest. Usually I suppress it and go about my business. Business as usual: Marcia back on the high dive; Florence King back on her blanket on the beach—but everything different. Marcia and Florence King are seeing a therapist twice a week. Marcia and I are friends, now. She waves to me out at the pool, she smiles. The old people's eyes pop out. I wave and smile, too. We sometimes arrange to walk on the beach and talk later in the day.

Hard to believe. I hardly believe it. It's so completely weird I can't even write a poem about it. I haven't written a poem in weeks. I don't even *want* to write one. I don't want to sit in my lifeguard stand and think. I don't want to play the sad songs of Joan Baez. Everything is changing in me. I have impulses that are new, startling to me. I want to climb up on the high dive in broad daylight and dive, right along with Marcia. I want to take my down jacket and slit it open and let the feathers blow away in the breeze. I don't want to swim in the dark, at night. I don't want to hide.

And yet I still hide. My twisted back is real. It won't blow away in the breeze. It's still there, and it's still my shame and misery.

Plunk, Plunk, Plunk. I could do without the noise. Why doesn't Simon go back to New York? He hasn't anything to do here anymore except annoy me.

As I think this, I am carrying some newspapers down to the incinerator and when I pass the door of the Storeroom, I kick it! Just like that—I kick it hard, and am halfway down the hall when I hear the door open.

"Did you want something?" Simon asks. "Was that you tapping?"

"No, it was just a little bird," I say, not even turning around.

"Hey," he says. "What's going on around here? Am I poison or something?"

"Something like that." I keep walking. Then I have to say something else—my head is ringing with the word "poison."

"Speaking of poison," I say, turning around, nearly shouting down the hallway so he can hear me, "if you hadn't abused the privilege my father trusted you with, Marcia wouldn't have tried to poison herself!"

"What are you talking about?" Now *he's* yelling down the hall, too.

"The key! The master key my father gave you so you could get into the Storeroom to build your stupid dulcimer. You gave it to Marcia!"

"What's this about poison?" he calls to me. "What are you talking about?"

"You're just lucky she didn't die, that's all."

I start walking toward the incinerator room. That's all I'm going to say to *him*!

But I hear him running after me. He grabs my elbow—and spins me around. "I don't know what you're talking about. I haven't talked to Marcia since she...got all mixed up with that guy..."

"Mr. Olympics..." I fill in for him.

"Yeah, whatever."

"I guess he hurt your feelings," I say, without pity.

"Any man would have been hurt, don't you think?"

"I don't know. I'm not a man. Thank heavens for that."

"Here, let me carry those newspapers for you," Simon says.

I wrench my arms away as he reaches out to take the load.

"I'm not helpless," I say.

"I wasn't suggesting you were. Can't I just help you?"

"You can help me by going home," I say. "Everything's turned upside-down since you came."

"But why?"

"Why do you think? Because you—just fell for Marcia. Like everyone else does! And you asked for special privileges, and then when you got them—you..."

"I what? I did what?" Simon shakes my arm. "Look, I want to know."

"You turned the pool lights on me!" Though I mean to say it in a rage, my voice cracks. Just remembering how I felt is too much for me. Tears fill my eyes, and he sees it happen.

"Hey," he says. "Hey. Look, why do you feel so bad? That was just a little joke, we didn't mean any harm by it."

He stops me now by blocking my way, and he takes the newspapers from my arms and sets them down on the floor of the hallway. Then he pulls me down with him, so we're both sitting with our backs against the wall.

"You didn't mean any harm," I repeat. I have to wipe my tears away with the sleeve of my down jacket.

"Hey, no, we didn't. It was just one of those crazy things people do. Marcia had this idea..."

"And you had the master key!"

"She convinced me to let her use it...."

"For a few days! Right? And then she had a copy made of it! And a few days ago I found her in Bernie Kriegel's apartment, trying to steal money for her mother's drug habit!"

"Jesus! I didn't know any of that!"

"Why would you know? You just were the cause of it! And right after I found her in Bernie's apartment, she used the key to open the Pool House and tried to kill herself by drinking chlorine!"

Simon has put his head down against his raised knees, and is covering his ears with his hands as if he doesn't want to hear any more of this.

"I didn't know," he says, finally. "That night—she just teased me and begged me for the key. You know how it is—you know how she is."

"I know how *you* are," I say. "Blinded by the light. By how gorgeous she is. By what a great swimmer she is."

"You're just as good a swimmer," Simon says, lifting his head and looking into my eyes. "That night we saw you in the pool, you were fantastic. You can really swim."

"Is that what you were thinking when you looked at me swimming?"

"What else would I have been thinking?"

I think of my back, all exposed, twisted, humped.

"You have terrific form," he adds. "I envy you."

Didn't he see my back? Is it possible he didn't even notice it?

"What about my back?" I finally ask him. This is something I absolutely have to know.

"What about it?"

"It's deformed," I say. I can't believe I've said that—I never said it out loud in my life before.

"I didn't notice anything."

"It's the most noticeable thing about me!" I cry.

"Maybe to you," he says. "Is that why you wear this jacket all the time?"

I nod.

"Maybe that's a mistake," he says. "I really didn't notice anything."

"I have scoliosis," I say. "Deformity of the spine."

"I have asthma," Simon says. "Constriction of the bronchial tubes."

"I thought you were perfectly healthy."

"I thought you were," Simon says.

This truly confuses me. Is it really possible that my hump didn't repel him? That he didn't even notice it? That it's not as monstrous as I imagine it to be?

"What do you do for your scoliosis?" Simon asks me.

"What do I do? Nothing! I hide it."

"Maybe there's something that can be done. I have different things I do for my asthma. Inhalators. Respiratory therapy sometimes. What does your doctor say?"

"I've never seen a doctor about it. Bones are different. You don't take medicine for a crooked bone."

"Maybe there's something that can be done."

"I doubt it."

"There's one thing you could do to make it easier for yourself." Simon says. "I mean—maybe it's none of my business, but you don't have to suffer in that hot jacket all the time, I mean, no matter how you look, or think you look, you have the right to be comfortable."

The way he says it makes me shiver inside, and the tears rise up again and spill over onto my cheeks. We've said too much, too fast, sitting here in the basement corridor. He's touched a nerve in me. I really can't talk about this anymore.

I stand up.

"Go ahead," Simon says. "I didn't mean to say more than I should have. I'll get rid of these newspapers for you. We'll talk later, if you want to."

Chapter Sixteen

But it's not Simon I want to talk to. I have been lying on my bed for two hours, trying to sort out my crazy feelings and wishing I could talk to someone about them. And the person I want to talk to is Marcia! *Not* Simon! I don't think Simon has had enough grief in his life to understand me. He seems, despite what his family has been through, untouched by real trouble. Somehow asthma doesn't seem to be in the same category with scoliosis and losing a mother (in my case), or incest and her mother's drug addiction (in Marcia's). I admit, that by his association with Gertie, his grandmother, Simon shares the grief of the Holocaust, but still, he's been spared having something happen up close. Something he's right there to feel! I'm feeling so sad and confused now that I want to talk to a person who can really understand. And that's

Marcia. Marcia, my enemy—now Marcia, my friend. Life never stops giving me little surprises.

So I drag myself out of bed and go out to find Marcia where I expect to find her: at the pool. She's finished doing her dives, and now she's doing laps. This time I have come out to the pool deck without the armor of my cleaning rag, without my trash bag; I have come out as if I have a right to be here because I live here and this is my pool, too. For the first time in my history at the Sea 'n' Surf Apartments, I sit down on a lounge chair and lean back. I let the sun fall on my face.

God—it's hot in my down jacket! The dark blue color of it absorbs the rays of the sun and takes them deep down to my bones. I bake like a chicken on a spit. Or maybe like a crow. I'm used to sweating. The humidity is always high in Florida. I sweat and suffer; it's easier than the suffering I'd have to experience if I took off my jacket. Or so I have always thought. But now I feel even hotter than usual. Or so it seems. I'm even tempted to unzip my zipper.

Marcia, cool as a sea lion, swims laps. The water spills off her back, her muscles ripple. She's a handsome sea animal. I no longer feel her beauty is hateful; it's simply what she has, what she *is*.

Yetta Korn is careful to stay out of Marcia's way. Today she's doing exercises at the side of the pool. She hangs on to the coping and kicks. She kicks up a white foam, and the cherries on her bathing cap rattle like crazy. She looks up and sees me watching her.

"How do I look, darling?" she asks me. "I'm firming my thighs. I want to be in shape for my wedding," she says.

Her *wedding*! She's grinning so happily, so joyously, that I want to ask *When? Where?* It's an effort not to answer her! My rule, that I must not ever talk to the old folks, is beginning to puzzle me. Why do I insist on it? Why shouldn't I speak to them if I want to?

Well, at least I can smile at Yetta. My rule doesn't cover smiling. Yetta, looking somewhat astonished at any response from me, winks gaily. A wedding! The groom in Yetta's plans has got to be Bernie Kriegel. Bernie! My face flushes at the thought of him and at what I know which I have got to keep a secret. At least it is not a *terrible* crime I am concealing. At least Marcia never actually stole a thing from his apartment.

Marcia swims, her strong arms cutting the water, her mouth turning up to gulp air, and then her face entering the water again. She loses herself in this, this anaesthetic balm, this aqua drug, this medication of dedication. I wish...

But there I go, wishing, envying. Envying! Envy is a mistake; I learn it every day, and I forget it just as fast. There is no one to envy; except maybe Simon. Simon, that calm, reasonable young man, down there in the Storeroom, plunking away on his dulcimer.

I unzip my zipper. Fancy that; the sky does not fall in. I only unzip it halfway. No one sends up rockets. No one points and hee-haws like a donkey. No one cries "Look at her!" Yetta keeps kicking. Marcia keeps swimming. Bernie keeps reading. The Canasta Ladies keep dealing cards. And there's my darling father, limping slowly along toward the Pool House, carrying the leaf skimmer. He doesn't even see me.

So I am not the center of the universe. Imagine that. Whatever made me think I was?

At the same instant, Gertie and Simon emerge from the door of the Game Room. She's got her arm linked firmly in his; it looks as if she's practically pulling him along. Simon's head is down. He probably doesn't want to see me. I'm sure he certainly doesn't want to see Marcia. But Gertie is dragging him along. Or no—rather, I see it now, she's leaning on him. Leaning quite heavily. And looking pale.

Simon leads her to a chair right next to mine and holds her while she slowly settles herself into it. She's let down her guard for some reason. She actually looks like an old woman.

"Gertie!" one of the Canasta Ladies calls from across the pool. "Come play? We're one short over here."

"No, no thank you, not today," Gertie says, but the wind carries her words away. They don't hear her. Simon has to call it out for her, "She says not today."

"Why not?"

"A little tired," Gertie says.

"She's a little tired," Simon repeats loudly for their benefit.

Gertie leans back and sighs. Her face is drained of color. She turns her head to the side and notices me.

"Good," she says. "You opened your jacket. It's about time, sweetheart."

Simon, luckily, doesn't hear her say this because he is already walking away, quickly, toward the door to the Game Room. Marcia, still swimming, hasn't even seen him. Nor has Bernie, still reading. Yetta is kicking away. Only Gertie and I know everything that's going on.

She grabs my hand. This is very strange—the power of her grip. It's not just a friendly touch. It's not the way a person who is talking to you will touch you casually.

Her hand is like a claw on me! I look at her and then I yell! "Simon! Simon!" He can't have gone far. She's turning blue. Gertie is turning blue and she's clutching my hand.

I scream his name again, and he appears. "Simon! Call the paramedics! Something's wrong with Gertie! Hurry, oh God, hurry!" I have a glimpse of my father coming toward us. Bernie is there. Yetta is dripping, jumping up and down at my feet. But all I can think of is that I will have to watch Gertie die. And I have never been so frightened in my life.

Chapter Seventeen

Four fireman, wearing red suspenders, blue shirts, yellow pants and high rubber boots—two of them carrying large red boxes—materialize at Gertie's side. Have we been waiting for them an eternity? Or only five minutes? I am on my knees, cradling Gertie in my arms as she tries to breathe. With all my concentration, I will her to breathe.

I feel hands on my shoulders; someone gently lifts me, moves me out of the way. The firemen take things out of their red boxes—machines, instruments, tubes, canisters. I recognize a blood pressure cuff, a stethoscope. Mainly I am watching Gertie's blue face; not the color of life. The pool, the ocean, the sky can be blue, as blue as they want it to be, but please—not Gertie's face. Oh please! Not blue skin on the sweet, funny, tough, beautiful face of Gertie!

No dying here. Please. No dying. Living is hard enough. But dying—dying is unthinkable! Impossible!

Medical things, mysterious things, scary things, are being done to Gertie, and someone is holding my hand. Who? It doesn't matter; the hand is warmth, assurance, comfort. I lean back and let my weight fall upon someone's body. Whose? It doesn't matter; the body is sweet as life. Someone else touches my hair while the firemen attach electrodes to Gertie's chest.

"Okay, stand back," the kneeling fireman says. He seems to be in charge. "Here we go: one, two, three."

Gertie arches up like a trapped animal trying to break free from its bonds.

"Once more!" The current surges through her, flings her upward.

"She's starting now," says the fireman. "We got her going."

"I think she'll be okay now," my father's voice whispers in my ear. I turn to see that I am leaning upon him. And beside him is Marcia, dripping wet in her red suit, almost as pale as my father. When she sees me looking at her, she reaches forward to squeeze my arm. And right next to me is Simon, with his arm out; at the end of it is my hand. Simon has been holding my hand through all of this!

Simon and I sit with Gertie and a paramedic in the ambulance as it races toward the hospital. We sit on a narrow bench, and the paramedic kneels beside her. He is monitoring her breathing, her pulse. Her skin is no longer blue. Not pink, but not blue. Pale, pale white. Her eyes are open. She even gives us a tiny, weak smile. The siren is deafening. I think it is making things much worse, scaring us even more. But Gertie has this small, grateful smile upon her face. Her wig has come off somewhere, and her white hair lies upon her head like fine thread.

My teeth are chattering—with cold, with fright. Simon takes my hand. Then, in the most amazing way, we turn toward each other and hug each other. I don't know why—it's relief, it's hope, it's human comfort. It doesn't matter what it is. We just do it.

And then, marvelously, Gertie speaks. She speaks to me. "I know your rule, *Feygele*," she says in a quivery soft voice. "I know your rule, darling, and you mustn't break it because of me, you don't have to say a word. But please ... would you hold my hand?"

"Oh God, of course! Of course I will!" I lean over the oxygen tubes, the electrodes, and grasp her hand tightly in mine. "And you'll be fine," I say at once. "You'll see you'll be just fine." I squeeze her hand very carefully. Simon leans forward and places his hand over mine, which is over hers.

"You're okay, Grandma," he says.

"You'll be good as new," I promise.

"You're breaking your rule, darling," Gertie reminds me. "Remember that day you came up to my apartment to show me the rules? That Simon shouldn't be with me? Well, aren't you glad he's with me? Such a good boy." She stops talking, closes her eyes. Her body convulses in a great shiver, and the paramedic pulls the blanket up over her shoulders. He places his fingers over his lips to show me, *No more talking.*

"Here, Gertie," I say, almost crying. I slowly take off my down jacket. I lay it on top of the blanket. "Maybe this will warm you up a little."

In the waiting room, we meet the same nurse who had been there the day I came in with Marcia.

"You like it here, or what?" she says kindly. "You planning to move in?"

After Gertie has been wheeled away on the gurney, Simon and I sit together on an orange plastic couch. We don't talk; he leans back, and his long legs stretch out in front of him. It seems as if hours pass. Finally he suggests we buy something hot to drink from the vending machine. He takes several quarters out of his pants pocket and holds them toward me in the palm of his hand. I pick them up, one by one.

"I'll get it," I say. "Coffee or hot chocolate."

"Whatever you have."

"Fine." I drop two coins in the slot and push the button for hot chocolate. While the cup falls into place, while the steaming drink fills the cup to the brim, I see myself in the mirror of the vending machine. I look like any girl, wearing a yellow cotton blouse and blue jeans. My down jacket is gone, it has disappeared with Gertie, but I am still myself. I haven't been transformed into anything amazing—I'm not suddenly a monster, certainly not an angel. I am just myself, in a hospital waiting room, getting something hot to drink.

Why have I always given my jacket so much power? Allowed it to be so important? Clutched it to me like a dying man clutches a lifesaver? I think of Gertie clutching it now, perhaps hanging on to it for dear life, up there in the intensive care unit. God, let it save her. Let her fly away from death on its feathers. I don't really need it, do I?

I hold one cup in my hand, insert the other two coins in the machine. I watch the insulated cup fill with the foamy, creamy hot chocolate. It looks delicious to me; my mouth waters. Simon is watching me from across the room. I am sure he can see my back clearly—it's facing him. As I turn to carry the drinks toward him, I glance over my shoulder and see my own back in the mirror. It's there, all right. My spine is all wrong, it's crooked, it's really there, ruined as ever, curved as a hook. But I think, *So what? So what? I'm alive and well. I'm here with Simon. And we hugged each other. And I'm about to drink this sweet, wonderful, steaming hot chocolate!*

Chapter Eighteen

The doorbell of our apartment rings early the next morning. Marcia is standing in the hallway, wearing a blue linen dress. "I can't talk now," she says, adjusting her purse over her shoulder, "because I'm on the way with my mother to the therapist's office, but I wanted to know if you've heard anything about Gertie."

My father is at the kitchen table in his bathrobe; he's eating bran cereal and reading a magazine. His head comes up now; he's listening to us.

"I called the hospital this morning. They said her condition is stable. I think that means she's okay. I'm going over there in a little while with Simon. We're only allowed to visit five minutes every hour as long as she's in the intensive care unit."

"Thank heaven she didn't die," Marcia says.

Out of the blue, my father says, in a deep voice, "She's an old woman, she's lived a very long life. No one lives forever."

I don't know what he means by this. Is he trying to get us ready for something? Or is he thinking of my mother? Or of his buddy in Viet Nam? Then he surprises me even more. He says to Marcia, "How's your mother?"

"She's okay," Marcia says. "She's doing really well."

"Tell her I have that article for her," my father says.

Article? For her? What is he talking about?

Marcia and I look at each other; he's gone back to reading his magazine. She shrugs her shoulders, and I shrug mine. We smile. Marcia stands there looking at me, and I have a fleeting feeling of fear that I'm naked. My jacket is gone. My shoulders, one lower than the other, are right there, out in the open. But I get hold of myself; I'm dealing with this. Simon told me, in the long hours of our wait at the hospital, that he's glad I gave his grandmother my down jacket; that he hopes I don't take it back. That I'll be fine, just fine, without it.

He said it again just after we had been allowed in to talk to Gertie once more: she told us not to worry, she was fine; she wanted us to go home and enjoy ourselves. We had been walking back toward the Sea 'n' Surf when I saw three disabled people: a young woman in a wheelchair, an old man with a walker, a child with crutches. And there I was, nearly perfect, with just a little glitch in my spine, a bump, a twist, a curve. Hardly anything. And Simon had said to me: "See? Everyone has something."

Marcia says she'll see me later. She walks off with what *she* has—perfect posture, exquisite body—and I know I can't really trick myself this way. My deformity is not "hardly anything." I just have to keep remembering that it's not the end of the world.

"What kind of article do you have for Marcia's mother?" I ask my father, interrupting him, which I hardly ever do.

"It's about a woman who recovered from a cocaine habit," my father says matter-of-factly. "We got to talking about it on the beach the other day."

"You did?" I ask.

My father looks up at me, holding a spoonful of cereal halfway to his mouth, and smiles. "She's a nice woman, Florence," he says. "Her life is full of troubles, though. Funny, how I never thought much of her in all these years."

"I never thought much of Marcia, either," I say, as if he doesn't know.

"Well, it just goes to show you...." he suggests, and goes back to eating and reading.

Simon knocks at our door soon afterward. Even our door is changing. No one ever used to knock on it—except to call my father to fix whatever was broken. But no one ever knocked on it to talk to us, to check with us, to visit us. We're becoming a regular social center now.

"She's doing fine," Simon says. "But they're going to put in a pacemaker. Her heart isn't making the right number of beats; the electrical system is all messed up. But once they put in the pacemaker, her heartbeat will be regular and reliable."

"Is it dangerous?"

My father, who is still at the table, pipes up again. "Is eating dangerous?" he says. "Is breathing? The nature of life is dangerous." I wonder why he's so talkative all of a sudden.

Simon says to him, "The essence of being alive is that you could be dead at any instant."

My father looks at this boy as if he's met a genius. He approves of Simon. "That's right," he says. "You got it." But instead of sounding grim, he sounds cheery. As if Simon discovered the right answer to the question my father's been carrying around with him all his life.

"We're going to visit Gertie," I tell my father.

"Want to come?" Simon asks.

Little does he know my father never leaves the premises except to go the lumberyard, the home improvement center and, occasionally, the supermarket.

"Yeah—why not?" he says.

This is really bizarre. Because Gertie has had a heart attack, everyone is acting extremely peculiar. Simon and Marcia are knocking at my door, my father is clipping articles for Florence King—and now he's limping off to get dressed.

We are going to drive in my father's truck to the hospital. Before we get in, Simon admires the wooden toolbox my father built in the bed of the pickup. It has smooth-sanded sides, perfectly fitted joints and a combination lock.

"This is first-rate," Simon says. "You ought to be making furniture."

"One of these days I intend to," my father says. "It's just one of those things I never got around to."

"Maybe, if you have time, you'd like to see my dulcimer," Simon suggests. "Maybe you could give me some pointers. On using glue—I've had some trouble there."

"You've got to use the clamps right," my father says. "I'll come down one of these days and have a look."

Simon looks at me as we drive along; I'm sitting in the middle. "You can come down to the Storeroom, too," he says. "I'll play a song for you."

Gertie is pinker today. That deadly waxen color is gone from her face. She's sitting up in bed, but she has an oxygen tube in her nose and an IV needle in the top of her left hand.

"Sorry for all the fuss," she says. "Sirens, firemen, all that attention." She seems pleased, if somewhat astonished, to see my father. She says to him, "And after all that trouble you went to, putting in alarm bells in my apartment—I had to go and have my heart attack outside, by the pool."

"Don't worry about it," my father says. His face reddens a little. "We're all happy you're feeling better now."

"Miracles of modern science," Gertie says. "They're putting in a pacemaker tomorrow. It runs on a little tiny battery; imagine that. If this had happened to me ten or so years ago it would have been *toodloo, Gertie*."

"I have a message for you from Yetta Korn," Simon says. "It's a secret." Simon goes to the bed, bends down and whispers into Gertie's ear.

"Really?" Gertie says. "She wants me?"

"She really does."

"Just imagine. At my age—Maid of Honor."

"I guess it would be Matron," Simon corrects her.

"They don't know?" Gertie asks.

"I know," I say. "Yetta let it slip the other day when she was doing her pool kicks."

"Know what?" my father asks.

"Yetta is getting married!" Gertie says.

"Who to?"

"To the king of Wall Street," Gertie says, and laughs.

Simon and I glance at each other. Luckily, just then, the door opens and a doctor and nurse come in.

"Time's up," the nurse says. "You've had more than your five minutes."

"Just one second," Gertie says. She reaches up and plucks the sleeve of the doctor's white coat. "Doctor Gold," she says, "I have a favor to ask of you."

"Why don't you wait till your visitors leave, and then we can talk?" he says. He's a tall, young doctor with a sweet face. I love his eyes; they're very kind.

"Well, I can't do that," Gertie says, "because it's about one of my visitors. *Feygele*, come stand by me."

My father and I exchange a brief look, and I go over to Gertie's bedside. She takes me by the arm.

"This young woman, Doctor Gold, has a problem that's been making her miserable. Turn around," she instructs me, giving me a little push.

I don't budge. My breath catches in my throat. What is she getting at?

"She has a little problem with her back," Gertie says. "I wish you'd take a look."

The doctor is already taking a look. So is Simon. So is my father. I feel as if *I* am going to have a heart attack.

I feel the doctor reach out and run his two fingers down my spine.

"You do have a little problem here," he says. "What has your doctor told you about this?"

"I don't have a doctor," I say. I glance around, looking for my down jacket. If only I can find it, put it on, disappear into it, I won't have to stand in the glare of so many curious eyes.

"I'm her father," my father says to the doctor. "And it's true, she doesn't have a doctor for this...condition she has..."

"Scoliosis is what it's called," Dr. Gold says. "And this is a pretty severe case; if you'd caught it when she was younger, we could have done a good deal for her. In fact, we still can—but it's a little trickier at this age."

"What can be done?" Simon says. It's as if everyone here is my mother and father. "Is it surgery?"

"Surgery is nothing," Gertie pipes up from her bed. "I'm having it tomorrow. I'm happy as could be they can do something."

Now the doctor is turning me around as if I'm on a revolving wheel. "I'm going to get you an appointment with our scoliosis specialist," he says. "That is, if it's okay with you."

"It's fine," my father says. "I wish we had looked into this years ago."

"Why doesn't someone ask me if it's fine with me?" I cry out.

"Well, is it?" Dr. Gold asks kindly.

I open my mouth to answer, but Simon says the words. "Sure it's fine with her," he says. "Why wouldn't it be?"

Chapter Nineteen

Acute adolescent idiopathic scoliosis is what I have. Dr. Reston, the scoliosis expert, and Dr. Gold took twenty-four X rays and measured every bone in my back before they decided what the best course of treatment would be. They said my "iliac crest has met the sacroiliac junction and firmly seals to the ilium," which simply means that I've more-or-less stopped growing and I can have the surgery very soon.

They want to do a "Harrington Rod" surgery on me. They showed my father and me pictures of what the rod looks like: it's just a long, metal pole with what looks like some nuts and bolts at either end, invented by a doctor named Harrington, and it will be attached to my spine by two hooks which connect to my vertebrae. They'll have to take bone shavings from my hips and graft them between the rod and the bone so that all the parts can calcify into one rigid, upright support. I'll have to be in a body cast for three to six months. And after that, I'll have a straight back! I won't be able to do any backbends, ("You may have to give up your plans to be a ballerina," Dr. Reston said), but he assured me I would be able to bend forward from the waist, and that should allow me all the motion I need.

The doctors told us so many things I can hardly remember all of them, but mainly they said I can live a normal life, I can have children, I can swim and dance and do everything! And best of all, my back won't get worse, my ribs won't get twisted to the side any farther, I won't have a huge hump and I won't have my lung compressed by my ribs.

"Is the surgery dangerous?" I ask Dr. Reston, and he opens a medical book and shows me a long, italicized sentence. Then he writes it down on a piece of paper with his black marker pen (it takes him a long time) and hands it to me: *"Scoliosis surgery done by a team of experts in a modern hospital doing a large volume of these operations is statistically safer for a patient than an automobile trip from New York to Florida, a trip thousands of families make every week!"*

"I want you to read this every night before you go to bed," he says. "Until the day of surgery."

After my medical exam is over, we get in the elevator and go up to the eleventh floor: the cardiac recovery unit. Gertie's nurses know me by now—I've been there every day since Gertie's surgery. They smile at my father, who nods shyly and follows me down the hall. Gertie is sitting up in bed, reading. She's wearing a pink, quilted bed jacket.

"I'm having the surgery for sure, Gertie," I say. "It's definite. At the end of August."

"You'll be so happy, afterward," Gertie says. "It's a miracle we got the doctor to look at you. So maybe my heart attack was a blessing in disguise."

"I wouldn't go so far as to say that!" I tell her.

"Oh, but I would. When good comes of bad, we know we're doing the right thing. The real tragedy is to let the bad take you over. It's our duty in life to pick up the pieces and go on." Gertie looks right into my eyes when she says this, and I remember the photographs in her apartment, her *first* family. "And guess what?" she asks.

"What?"

"I'm going to be president of the Pacer Club. I went to my first meeting this morning. They wheeled me down to attend."

"It sounds like a running club," my father remarks with a smile.

"Oh no, oh no—we all have pacemakers," Gertie says. "Here—want to look at mine?"

I don't know if I do, but she's already untying her bed jacket and tugging down her nightgown slightly. I look at my father, and he looks at me. Gertie shows us her scar, the reddened skin, and under the skin, a little round raised circle.

"That's it," she said. "That little thing! It saves my life every minute of the day and night. It just keeps tick-tocking away, keeping me hale and hearty!"

"Does it last forever?"

"Long enough," Gertie says. "Ten to fifteen years—which, at my age, I'd say, is as good as forever."

On the way home I try to imagine what it must be like to have surgery, to lie down and turn yourself over to the knife. To be unconscious. Vulnerable. Alone, with no one who loves you to hold your hand, in a big, scary operating room. I imagine myself feeling awful pain. I imagine myself in a body cast ("Possibly for as long as six months!" Dr. Reston warned me). But, still, I can't scare myself very much. All this just doesn't strike me as scary! What *is* scary is the thought of myself hunched over in my down jacket for the rest of my life, a miserable creature, a bird with clipped wings, the Crow who will never show her face in the world in daylight!

"I could die in surgery," I say to my father, testing him. "Aren't you worried?"

"We could all die," he answers. "We all *will*. No, I'm not worried. I'm relieved we can do this, that you can have this surgery, that the doctors can help fix your spine, fix it as much as they can. I'm just sorry, Faye, really sorry, that I didn't figure this out years ago. I knew something was going on with you, but—well, I don't know. I didn't want to lean on you too hard. Your life was hard enough without your mother. Maybe I was afraid to bring it out into the open...."

"My mother would be very happy today," I assure him. "She'd be happy for me. And I'm happy," I say. "I'm really feeling very happy."

"I hope you can forgive me," my father says, and for some reason, suddenly, like a lunatic, I laugh out loud. This is beginning to sound like a soap opera, with my father talking about my mother who died young and asking me to forgive him. Of course I do. And I hope he forgives me for all those hours and days and months I barely talked to him, didn't smile at him, hated the world. Because he lost my mother, too. He's been alone and aching, too.

So instead of talking and saying embarrassing words, I just hold my hand out toward him, and he takes it in his and hangs onto it, holds it real tight in his big hand there on the seat of his pickup truck. And we drive all the way back to the Sea 'n' Surf that way, holding hands, me and my father, the Crow and the Shadow, both of us smiling.

Chapter Twenty

"You saved my life," Marcia says to me. "You saved my mother's, too. How can we ever repay you?"

We are sitting in the lifeguard station, where we always end up after our run. Marcia wants me to get in better shape before my surgery. She wants me to increase my lung capacity, develop better muscle tone in my body. She supervises me while I swim twenty laps every morning, and then in the afternoon, she runs with me along the beach.

"You *are* repaying me," I say. "Think of it this way. If I had to go to a gym and hire an expert like you to work out with me, it would cost me a million dollars."

"I'm serious," she says. "In the last few weeks, everything in my life has turned around."

"Everything in mine, too," I say. "Funny, how life is."

"My mother is almost human. She's not catatonic anymore. She doesn't just conk out on the beach every day. I mean, we talk now! We talk with the therapist, and then we come home and talk some more. We talk lots about my father, who we never even mentioned before. And we talk about my grandfather, who's always handing over money with strings attached; you can have this much if you do such and such. My mother's tired of that, and she realizes it's her fault, that she's always been so dependent on him. She's talking about getting a job, doing something to take care of herself."

"Well, in a way it must be nice to be supported by someone who's rich," I say. "We live pretty close to the bone, as my father says."

"Your father!" Marcia says. She looks out to sea, and the wind blows her blond hair back from her face. Her profile is clean and perfect, like her dives. "I'd give a lot for a father like yours."

"How come?"

"Well, he's so... laid back or something. I mean, he sits around in our kitchen and he doesn't say much, but there's a calm about him..."

"He sits around in your *kitchen*?"

"All the time, lately."

"What's broken in there?"

"Nothing's broken. He visits my mother."

"He *visits* her?"

"Why are you looking so odd? It's not against the law for him to visit her, is it?"

"Well, he just never visited anyone before."

"I told you, Faye—everything's changed lately. I'm different, you're different, my mother's different, your father's different."

"It's because of Gertie," I say. "She's our fairy godmother. She waved her magic wand or something."

"She's amazing," Marcia says. "I want to be just like that when I'm almost eighty."

"Only Simon isn't different," I say. "I mean—he's the only one not changing his life in some big way, like we are."

"Yes, he is," Marcia says.

"He is?"

She nods. A funny little smile comes over her mouth, and my heart sinks. She's going with him or something, I think suddenly. It's not over. Maybe she's going to tell me they're getting married.

"How is he changing his life?" I almost don't want to hear. My feelings about him are so powerful, I can hardly think his name without getting wild vibrations in my chest. I've been trying to steel myself; soon the summer will be over, and he'll be on his way back to New York. That's it, that's life, those are the hard facts. In the fall, I'll be in the hospital in my body cast, and Simon will be wandering around in Central Park.

"He's moving down here," Marcia says.

I try to control myself. I don't want to keel over and break my neck falling out of the lifeguard stand.

"What do you mean by that?"

"I mean, he's staying. He and Gertie are moving into a two-bedroom in the building, so he can have his own room. He likes Florida. He wants to stay around with Gertie and keep an eye on her. He'll go to school here for his senior year."

"How do you know all this?"

"Oh, my mother knows. Your father told her."

"My father knows this?"

"Well, he's the manager. He's *got* to know."

"He never told *me*."

"Maybe he didn't think it has much to do with you."

I am speechless. *Not have much to do with me!*

Marcia says, "Men are sort of thick-brained. Your father might not know how you feel about Simon."

Now I stare out to sea. My head is spinning. Simon staying on! Simon living here in the Sea 'n' Surf for another year!

"In case you want to know," Marcia says, "Simon and I didn't really get it on. I mean, we got something started, but we didn't get very far. He's a nice guy and all that, but he's not really for me. He's too dreamy. He's building that whatever-it-is down in the Storeroom, and he plays whatever-he-plays on it."

"Folk ballads," I say.

"Yeah, whatever," Marcia says. "I could understand a guy building an electric guitar or something to play heavy metal or hard rock on, but Simon's in some other universe..."

"He's really staying another year?"

Marcia pokes me. "You are not dreaming. This is the real world. Tune in, Faye. This is a fact."

I stand up and jump down into the sand. "Let's run some more," I tell Marcia. "I feel as if I need to run."

I really feel as if I need to fly. The sun is wonderful, warming my back, my whole body. I'm wearing running shoes and shorts and a cotton shirt. Without my down jacket I am really free as a bird. I don't know what happened to it—it just disappeared. It never came back from the hospital. I have a feeling Gertie got rid of it. I never asked. I don't ever want to see it again.

Marcia is ahead of me, her strong feet pushing against the sand near the water's edge. She leaves little footprints which I try to step into. She runs in a straight line, crushing seaweed and shells underfoot.

"Getting tired?" she calls over her shoulder.

"That's okay," I gasp. "I need this."

"You're going to be so strong," she yells to me, "that you'll have the fastest recovery on record."

Chapter Twenty-one

Simon is getting interested in scoliosis. Just as I'm getting less interested in my back, he's getting more interested in it. I want to give up thinking about it, and he wants to study the problem. I want to think ahead to when my back will be straight as a ramrod, and he wants to take me to the library to read up on it.

We are on the bus, going to the Miami Beach library. Simon says he hears the University of Miami has a good medical school. "I may go into medicine," he says. "Look what they did for Gertie with that little pacemaker. Extended her life by ten or twenty years—who knows?"

"Doctors get called in the middle of the night," I say. "They never get any sleep."

"You can take half the calls," he says.

"What?"

"We can share a practice. Then you'll sleep some nights and I'll sleep some nights."

Is he crazy? "What are you talking about? I'm not going to be a doctor."

"What are you going to be?"

"Maybe a poet." But as I say it, I realize that's not what I want to be. Poets have to think and wonder and agonize and suffer. I've done that for years. I've sat and stared at the ocean and cried quite enough. I want to be busier when I'm an adult.

"I thought I might be a dulcimer-player," Simon says, "but I've given up that idea. Unrealistic."

"No money in it," I add.

"That too. Not that money is everything."

"I never said it was."

"Neither did I," Simon says, a little defensively.

This is heavy stuff we're getting into. I thought we were just going to take a nice ride down Indian Creek Drive to the library.

"How's Gertie?" I ask.

"She's fantastic. She's going to be fitted today for her Matron of Honor bathing suit."

"Bathing suit?"

"Yetta Korn's wedding. Didn't you hear? The ceremony is going to be in the middle of the pool." Simon's face begins to crack up. "The rabbi is going to stand on a floating raft and perform the ceremony!" he says.

"And the bridesmaids?"

"The Canasta Ladies—they're going to wedge themselves into Styrofoam donuts and paddle around making a graceful heart-shaped design around Bernie and Yetta."

"You're kidding me," I say.

"Wait and see," Simon says. He picks up my hand in his and twines his fingers in mine. "Wait and see," he says. "This will be the wedding of the century."

In the library, I'm reading an article in *Mademoiselle* on ten ways to wear curly hair when Simon slides the book he's reading under my nose. "Look at this," he says. "They're developing electrospinal instrumentation to correct scoliosis by applying a mild electric current to the convex side of the scoliotic curve."

"Good," I say. I push the book away.

"I wonder how you got your curve," he says. "Genetic—that's possible. Do you know if your mother had it?"

"No," I say. I don't want to talk about my mother.

"Sometimes there's paralysis or injury to the back muscle on one side of the spine, so it doesn't pull with as much power on the spine as the muscle on the other side does."

"Very interesting," I say. I show him *my* article. "Girls with curly hair can wear it short and curly or long and curly. Or short and curly on top and long in the back, or long and curly on top and short in the back."

"Why can't you be serious, Faye? Don't you want to learn as much as you can about your condition? Maybe there was trauma to your embryo in your early formative period."

"Right!" I say. "I had plenty of trauma in my early formative period, Simon. My father got shot up in Viet Nam. My mother died. Don't you understand about suffering? People who have suffered may not want to think about it day and night. But you wouldn't know much about suffering, would you?"

Simon's mouth practically falls open right there. But he doesn't talk any more to me about scoliosis. He reads his book and I read my magazine, and eventually we take the bus back to the Sea 'n' Surf.

Gertie, it's true, is working on her Matron of Honor dress. At least it's not a bathing suit! I point this out to Simon when we get back to the apartment, and I smile at him, but he's not in a smiling mood. He seems stung by what I said in the library, and I'm sorry I said it.

Gertie is looking really well. The color is high on her cheeks, she's peppy, she's in charge of her life again.

"I'm glad to see you and Marcia are turning out to be nice little friends," she says. "Remember that day, when we were looking out the window, when I told you it's not all sugar and spice for her?"

"I remember, yes—and you were right."

"I don't want a medal for being right, darling. I just wanted you to see the knocks are handed out pretty equal."

"More or less," I say, glancing over at Simon, who is listening to us.

Suddenly Simon gets off the couch, goes to the drawer in the china cabinet where the old picture album is kept. He unlocks the drawer quickly, as if he has done it many times recently.

"What are you doing, Simon?" Gertie says. "Close the drawer, please."

But Simon has lifted out the crumbling album.

"You know that's not allowed!" Gertie says in alarm. "Put that away, Simon."

"I want to show it to Faye," Simon says. "She thinks I've had an easy life."

"You have," Gertie says angrily. "Close the drawer, Simon. That's my drawer. My private things are in it."

"This isn't private, Grandma," Simon says, and I hear a frightening quiver in his voice. "This isn't just yours, Grandma."

"Then whose is it?" Gertie asks. "I don't know anyone else whose family is in that album."

"*My* family!" Simon says, and there's an anger in his voice I've never heard. "Do you think that what happened in the camps just happened to you? Even though I wasn't even born then, don't you know every bit of it happened to me? It happened all over again to your second family. It happened to my mother! The children of survivors don't get away from the Holocaust, Grandma! Believe me, neither do the grandchildren. They live it, day and night. They think about it all the time. They feel guilty that they were allowed to be born, to grow up, to live."

Simon holds the album open toward me, and I bow my head. No one knows I have already seen it. "This is my grandmother's first family, Faye. They were killed in the concentration camp."

Gertie is no longer sewing on her gown. She is crying. Simon looks shocked at what he has started. He goes to her and puts his arms around her. He is crying, now, also.

I get up quietly and let myself out of the apartment. As I walk down the long hall, I begin crying, too. I whisper out loud, as if I am conjugating a verb for school, "I suffer, you suffer, we all suffer."

Chapter Twenty-two

After dinner, I knock on the door of the Storeroom and enter when Simon calls out, "Come in." He's sweeping up some wood shavings from the floor. They're fragrant—they remind me of the piney woods. When he sees it's me, he keeps right on sweeping, his head down. He looks very sad.

"Simon, I'm sorry," I say. I'm not sure how to go about this. I haven't had much practice in apologizing to anyone. I never felt I was in the wrong before. I have a lot to learn—I can see that.

"That's okay," he says. "Maybe you had a point."

"I never should have said what I said. It's just a little hard for me to give up being Queen of Pain or something. I've carried that idea around with me so long."

"It doesn't matter," Simon says. "We're not in some kind of contest to prove who's suffered the most. I guess we just have to deal with whatever comes along. So don't worry."

"Okay," I say, "and don't you worry."

He looks worried anyway. "I'm all finished in here," he says. "I can give your father back his key now."

I look around. The room is clean, except for the little pile of wood shavings at his feet. He sweeps them into a neat triangle. On the work bench is the completed dulcimer. I've never seen one up close before; it's a little like a lute, a little like an autoharp. It has a very short neck and a graceful, almost feminine shape. Four heart shapes are carved into the wood, two at either end on each side of the strings.

"Listen," Simon says. "You know I was thinking of moving down here. But now I'm thinking of going back to New York."

"Oh no! Don't!" I cry, before I can stop myself. "Please don't do that!"

"I'm all mixed up now," Simon says. "I was planning definitely to stay on for next year. I worked it all out with my parents; I wrote for my school records to be sent down. Only now I don't know…"

"What don't you know?" My heart is lurching like crazy. I've been counting on this so much I think I will die if he doesn't stay.

"I don't know if Gertie wants me around."

"Of course she does!"

"Well then, maybe you don't."

"Me?"

"Who else is here?"

"I want you around, Simon. *Believe me.* I want you around more than anything!"

"Well, I think maybe we'd get on each other's nerves or something."

"Simon, if you moved back to New York, I'd die of misery. Talk about suffering! I don't think I'd survive it. I need you!"

Simon seems to consider what I said. "Do you need me to see you through your operation?"

"No! Of course not! I can handle *that*. I need you just to be with me, just to see me, just so I can see *you*. I'm not worried about my operation."

"I thought you were."

" 'It's safer than a trip from Florida to New York, a trip which many families take every week'—I'm quoting my doctor."

"If I stay here, I'll be burning all my bridges behind me."

"You mustn't forget Gertie. She wants you here. She adores you."

"What about you?"

"Do I adore you? Give me a little time. I don't go around adoring anyone so fast."

"I didn't mean that."

Simon is really red in the face. He lifts the dulcimer off the work bench and sits down, laying it across his lap. Out of his pocket he takes a long, black feather and begins to pluck at the strings.

"What kind of bird did you get that from?"

"I found it on the beach. Maybe a gull."

"I think it's from a crow," I say.

"A crow," Simon muses.

"I used to be one," I say.

"Crow no more," he says, and begins to play a song and sing. The words are about a girl named Shady Grove who has cheeks as red as the blooming rose and eyes of the deepest brown. Simon sings, in a sweet, deep voice, looking right at me, "You are the darling of my heart, stay till the sun goes down."

When the sun does go down, we walk together to the lifeguard stand, and Simon and I climb up. We sit on its sandy seat, smelling the salt spray, letting the balmy wind stroke our faces.

The deepest feeling in me now is peace. I am quiet and still and peaceful deep inside me, where there used to be a tremendous churning and shaking. So much lies ahead—not just my surgery or my promised year with Simon, but something else, even better: my future—a huge sweet thing, like the moon which is just coming up, silvery and lighted and shaped in the most excellent way.

Simon is experiencing this, too—I can feel it in the warmth of his hands, which are holding both of mine. We watch the moon rise, first just a little glow on the far edge of the ocean, and then a glimmer of silver, coming toward us, like fish riding over the waves right to our feet. The brilliant globe rises straight over the waves, coming up with such certainty and power that we know we can count on it for the rest of our lives.

Simon puts his forehead against mine, then presses his cheek against my cheek, then his nose against my nose, then his lips against my lips. I feel as if our faces fit into the face of the moon, perfectly.

We sit in the darkness and hold each other for a long time. We don't speak. We just *are*. After a while Simon rests his head against my shoulder and closes his eyes. With my finger I trace the shape of his eyebrows, feel the feathery curve of his eyelashes. I hear a song start in my heart: *You are the darling of my heart, stay till the moon goes down.*

Chapter Twenty-three

Marcia has been busy all morning stringing red and white balloons from the top of the diving board to the tops of the cabanas. Wearing her little yellow shorts and a yellow halter top, she runs up and down the steps of the diving board without even looking, without holding on. Then she does the same with the ladder, moving it from place to place as she ties up the balloons. Her balance is perfect. Her mother, Florence, is unrolling a thick, white satin ribbon from a cardboard spool; my father has the loose end, and she's directing him.

"That's right," Florence King says. "Let's loop it from one beach chair to another, all around the whole pool." She's looking much better; the circles around her eyes are gone, she's gained a little weight. Her unnaturally dark suntan has faded, and her skin looks almost healthy. She looks at my father and smiles; he grins back. Maybe he's embarrassed, holding a white satin ribbon in his big hands. He looks funny with it—standing there in his jeans and his old shirt. But he looks happy, too—embarrassed and pleased at the same time.

The Canasta Ladies have been painting a sign in red poster paint which they plan to tape onto Bernie's car:

JUST MARRIED!!!

Other tenants of the Sea 'n' Surf are bustling about, sweeping the pool deck, dusting the diving board, placing little vases of hibiscus blossoms on card tables they've brought up from the Game Room.

Simon is down in the Storeroom practicing the wedding march on his dulcimer. He's worried that its tone is too soft to carry very far, especially if there's a breeze coming off the ocean, but I told him not to worry. An accordion would be louder, I assured him, but much less tasteful.

The Miami sky is at its picture-postcard best—a brilliant blue, with great puffy white clouds rising in the air like castles. The ocean is a deep greeny-blue, flicked with foamy wavelets. Gulls swoop and skim, flying against the sun. It's a magnificent day, the best kind of day for a wedding.

I'm polishing the silver rectangle of the water fountain. I'm kneeling and rubbing the sides of it with a soft, white towel. I can see myself reflected in the mirror of stainless steel—there I am, wearing (just like Marcia!) shorts and a halter top. I can see the twisted shape of my back when I turn sideways, but it seems a natural presence to me now, like the palm tree down on the beach which grows slightly tilted to the side. It's not perfect by any means, but it's interesting. It's a variation. It belongs here with everything else—in all the shapes that things come in.

My hair is a pleasant tangle of dark curls; I don't even wish for straight hair any longer. Simon says he loves my curls, he loves to bury his face in them and feel them tickle his nose.

I give a finishing touch to the fountain and stand up. Something—a shadow or movement in the building above me—catches my eye; it's Gertie, standing at her window. She's got the curtains pulled all the way back, and her figure stands perfectly still in the center of the window, like a sculpture. It's so still that I wonder if she could be made of marble. But then she sees me! She raises her hand slowly in a gentle wave. She stands there with her hand up, like the Statue of Liberty.

I throw her a great big kiss! Then I throw her three more, blowing them up to her window with the breath of love.

The wedding is about to begin! The guests are assembled and seated on the lounge chairs. The rabbi is present and waiting. Simon looks at me, and I nod. Trying to keep a straight face, he begins to pluck out the notes of the wedding march on his dulcimer.

The betrothed enter from the door of the Game Room. Bernie Kriegel, the groom, smoking a cigar as usual, is wearing leopard-skin swim trunks and has a black bow tie around his neck. His hairy, white chest is bare. Yetta Korn, the bride, is dressed to look like a ripe strawberry, with a little green leafy crown holding her bride's veil to the top of her head. Her red bathing suit is full of little black seeds. She has a short cape over her shoulders, made of white lace.

"This is too much," Simon whispers into my ear. "I'm not going to be able to carry on."

"Play!" I urge him. "Don't give up now!"

His shoulders shaking with laughter, Simon keeps strumming away.

Solemnly, Yetta Korn teeters forward on her high heels, holding to the arm of my father, who has been elected to give the bride away. My father is wearing a new blue shirt, his best blue jeans and his Viet Nam battle boots, newly shined. Behind Yetta, Gertie, dressed in a long, orange gown, has her arm looped in Bernie's arm as they walk slowly toward the diving board. She's giving the groom away.

The rabbi, a kind looking, bearded young man, looks as if he can't believe what he's gotten himself into. He is being ushered by Marcia, wearing a modest white bathing suit, to step onto a little wooden raft made to order by my father especially for the occasion. Simon and I look at each other; we can't believe this. Marcia steadies the raft in the pool and helps the rabbi to step onto it. He only loses his balance very briefly and rights himself by holding onto her shoulder. He quickly figures out that if he holds his feet apart and rocks gently from side to side, he can remain standing upright. I pray he can swim!

Yetta and Bernie slowly begin to ascend the steps to the top of the high dive. Gertie watches them anxiously; my father stands with his hands up, as if he will catch Yetta if she topples backward on her high heels and falls.

"*Whose idea was this?*" Simon whispers to me.

"It was a joint effort," I whisper back. "It took lots of planning; you don't just cook up a wedding like this in five minutes."

Bernie and Yetta pose graciously at the top of the high dive. Yetta unbuttons her lace cape and tosses it down, like a trapeze artist at a circus. Bernie looks longingly at his cigar and flips it away, into the wind. (Marcia runs to retrieve it and puts it out in an ashtray.)

"We need a drum roll now," I tell Simon.

He does the best he can, flicking his bird quill hard over the strings.

"Here she goes!" I say, hanging onto his arm.

Yetta dives straight down into the water. She dives very well, having been coached intensively during the last few days by Marcia. She surfaces, coming up like a tree, green leaves first. Then she moves aside for Bernie, who jumps in, holding his legs to his chest, displacing the water like a cannonball.

The rabbi, rocking for dear life on his raft, is doing his best to look serious and rabbinical.

"I never believed they would really go through with this," Simon whispers to me. "I thought they were just joking when I heard them talking about their plans."

"No joke," I say. "True love can overcome great obstacles."

"You bet," Simon says. No one is looking our way. He leans over and kisses me, softly, but also hard, right on the mouth.

Yetta and Bernie are now bobbing about in the water at the foot of the rabbi's raft. He's beginning to perform the ceremony, beginning to say the words. Bernie, who is not the best swimmer in the world, goes under for an instant, and emerges choking and sputtering. Marcia tenses, poised at the edge of the pool, ready to effect a rescue if necessary.

On dry land, Gertie and my father are standing together, arm in arm. I look around for Florence King and see her standing back a way, her hand on the back of a chair, looking quite pretty in a blue linen dress.

The rabbi is rocking on his raft and reciting the service, which he seems to have memorized. Bernie and Yetta are dog-paddling to stay afloat. Vows are exchanged above the burbling sound of water splashing softly. Promises to love, honor and cherish are made. From his pocket the rabbi extracts a small bottle of wine and a silver wine cup. Very nervously, he kneels on his raft and offers the cup, first to Yetta, then to Bernie. They drink. A little wine spills into the pool. From somewhere, Bernie produces a ring with a diamond as big as a baby coconut, and Yetta squeals with joy as he slips it on her finger.

"I now pronounce you man and wife," the rabbi says, and the bride and groom kiss, wetly and at length. Simon is cracking up. He buries his face in my shoulder, in order not to cackle out loud.

Then everyone is applauding, and the Canasta Ladies dive into the pool to do a little ballet with Yetta. Bernie scrambles out and looks around for his cigar. The Canasta Ladies form a giant, shaped heart, with Yetta in the center. It's very pretty; even Bernie smiles happily at the sight of his bride, buoyed up in her strawberry bathing suit. They blow kisses to each other, and then all the tenants of the Sea 'n' Surf begin throwing handfuls of popcorn into the pool.

"Rice sinks," I explain to Simon. "They wanted to be careful. When this is over, the popcorn can be skimmed right off the surface."

Marcia helps the rabbi to get safely off the raft. He kisses her in relief, truly thankful to be on firm ground.

Festivities ensue. A feast. Gertie's famous stuffed cabbage, roast sliced brisket, knishes, and on the dessert table honey cake and sponge cake.

Simon and I stuff ourselves. We kiss Yetta and shake Bernie's hand. My father and Florence King are busy talking. Gertie is sitting on a beach chair, and Marcia is perched on the foot of it. They are both merrily eating and laughing. Gertie is holding Simon's dulcimer in her lap for safekeeping.

"Think you and I could get away for a little while?" Simon asks. "I know this little place down the beach which is very private, if a little splintery."

"I know just the place you mean," I say, taking Simon's hand. We walk to the pool gate and slip out onto the sand.

I am dazzled by the brightness and beauty of the wide and endless beach stretched out before us.

* * * * *

Boarding school is rough!
What happens to a new student at
North Hill Academy is a crime....
Find out all the gory details in
another super ══CROSSWINDS
mystery by Glen Ebisch.

Angel in the Snow

It will materialize on your
bookstore shelves in February.

YOU CAN GET ALL THE CROSSWINDS BOOKS YOU MISSED...

To receive your Crosswinds books, complete the order form for *a minimum of two books*, clip out and send together with a check or money order payable to Crosswinds Reader Service (include 75¢ postage and handling) to:

In the U.S.
901 Fuhrmann Blvd.
P.O. Box 1396
Buffalo, N.Y. 14240-1396

In Canada
P.O. Box 609
Fort Erie, Ontario
L2A 5X3

QUANTITY	BOOK #	ISBN #	TITLE	AUTHOR	PRICE
☐	1	98001-9	Does Your Nose Get in the Way, Too?	Arlene Erlbach	$2.25
☐	2	98002-7	Lou Dunlop: Private Eye	Glen Ebisch	$2.25
☐	3	98003-5	Toughing it Out	Joan Oppenheimer	$2.25
☐	4	98004-0	Lou Dunlop: Cliffhanger	Glen Ebisch	$2.25
☐	5	98005-7	Guys, Dating and Other Disasters	Arlene Erlbach	$2.25
☐	6	98006-5	All Our Yesterdays	Stuart Buchan	$2.25
☐	7	98007-8	Sylvia Smith-Smith	Peter Nelson	$2.25
☐	8	98008-6	The Gifting	Ann Gabhart	$2.25
☐	9	98009-4	Bigger is Better	Sheila Schwartz	$2.25
☐	10	98010-8	The Eye of the Storm	Susan Dodson	$2.25
☐	11	98011-6	Shock Effect	Glen Ebisch	$2.25
☐	12	98012-4	Kaleidoscope	Candice Ransom	$2.25
☐	13	98013-2	A Kindred Spirit	Ann Gabhart	$2.25
☐	14	98014-0	The Right Moves	M. K. Kauffman	$2.25
☐	15	98015-9	Lighten Up, Jennifer	Kathlyn Lampi	$2.25
☐	16	98016-7	Red Rover, Red Rover	Joan Hess	$2.25
☐	17	98017-5	Even Pretty Girls Cry at Night	Merrill Joan Gerber	$2.25
☐	18	98018-3	Angel in the Snow	Glen Ebisch	$2.25
☐	19	98019-1	The Haunting Possibility	Susan Fletcher	$2.25
☐	20	98020-5	Dropout Blues	Arlene Erlbach	$2.25

Your Order Total $ _____

☐ (Minimum 2 Book Order)

Add Appropriate Sales Tax $ _____

Postage and Handling .75

I Enclose _____

Name _____

Address _____

City _____

State/Prov. _____ Zip/Postal Code _____

ATTRACTIVE, SPACE SAVING BOOK RACK

Display your most prized novels on this handsome and sturdy book rack. The hand-rubbed walnut finish will blend into your library decor with quiet elegance, providing a practical organizer for your favorite hard-or soft-covered books.

Only $9.95

Approximately 16" x 8" when assembled

Assembles in seconds!

To order, rush your name, address and zip code, along with a check or money order for $10.70* ($9.95 plus 75¢ postage and handling) payable to *Crosswinds*.

Crosswinds
Book Rack Offer
901 Fuhrmann Blvd.
P.O. Box 1396
Buffalo, NY 14269-1396

Offer not available in Canada.

*New York and Iowa residents add appropriate sales tax.